THE
NECESSITIES OF LIFE

GORDON SELF

 **FriesenPress**

Suite 300 – 852 Fort Street
Victoria, BC, Canada V8W 1H8
www.friesenpress.com

Copyright © 2014 by Gordon Self
First Edition — 2014

Photographer : Jon Popowich

All rights reserved.

Cover photograph of Vancouver's Downtown Eastside at night, and
chapter image of the silk scarf courtesy of Jon Popowich ©

This book is a work of fiction. Names, characters, places, and incidents either are
products of the author's imagination or are used fictitiously. Any resemblance to
actual events or locales or persons, living or dead, is entirely coincidental.

ISBN
978-1-4602-5189-8 (Hardcover)
978-1-4602-5188-1 (Paperback)
978-1-4602-5190-4 (eBook)

1. Fiction, Urban Life

Distributed to the trade by The Ingram Book Company

For Laura

ACKNOWLEDGMENTS

I wish to thank my colleagues and friends for their support in reviewing several manuscript drafts, and providing invaluable feedback as I developed the ideas and characters depicted in the story. I also want to acknowledge Dr. Geoff Cundiff and Br. Tom Maddix, CSC for their vision in establishing the first newborn safe haven in Vancouver, who in turn assisted us in the development of our own Angel Cradles in Edmonton. For Dr. Thomas Kerr in standing up and advocating for the needs of the disenfranchised in Vancouver's Downtown Eastside. And a word of thanks must go to Dr. Tom Gleason, for his friendship and additional clinical advice, as well as to Karen Macmillan, who posed the question to me and asked why not.

I am grateful to Bernadette Gasslein who encouraged my writing and foray into fiction. And, I am especially grateful for my adopted Vietnamese family, who inspired me to write this story after we reconnected after many years apart. While I played a role in helping them become settled in Canada in 1979, it is really this family who saved my life in which I owe the depth of gratitude.

Finally, I could not have written this novel without the unceasing loving support and belief of my family, my daughters, and especially, and always, my wife Theresa.

CHAPTER 1

Magda anxiously waited to enter, hoping she would be safe once inside. At least to find a seat in the corner somewhere, away from those now making their way up the front steps to the main door. She hung back from the sidewalk in the shadows, standing on the spongy wet lawn with no umbrella to shelter her from the rain. She feared if she stepped any closer someone might offer an umbrella, bringing her into view and exposing what she carried under her coat.

"They'd know if they saw me," she thought.

She kept telling herself she didn't belong, that she wasn't welcome, a message she had internalized long ago. It was better that way. Magda didn't want to be known, let alone risk someone actually caring for her. That would only lead to disappointment. Instead, she waited for the right moment, quickly stepping forward out from under the dark near the bottom of the stairs before anyone else came up the front sidewalk.

She trembled. Her shivering had increased since she left the train station. Magda had seen the building from the SkyTrain line which she rode sometimes just to get away from Luc, pretending she was working, risking a beating if she had no money to show for her absence. She could only do so if the last customer was generous, with either money or time. From the right side of the east-bound train at night, she often looked for the half-crescent panes of glass aglow as they neared the Joyce-Collingwood Station. The elevated train slowed just enough to give her a glimpse of the windows of light emanating from the church before her view was partially obstructed by the station platform walls. The church reminded her of the square building and glass arches that were such a familiar feature of her childhood parish in Poland. It was an ordinary concrete structure that people like Magda could go without standing out, remaining as invisible as she was on the street. This lone band of arched light seemed to call to her while she rested her head against the SkyTrain window, absently staring at passing neighbourhoods beyond her reach.

She was tempted once before to get off at Joyce-Collingwood and walk the couple of blocks to this church, but was too ashamed. Voices in her head kept her anchored to her seat.

"You're just a bitch. You're nothing without me. You hear me? Nothing."

Luc's voice was like an arrow. Instead of the church windows inviting her nearer, it seemed more like a bow, drawing Luc's words back in its arch and hurling it towards her, tearing through flesh and pinning her body to the world she could not escape.

It was always the same. As the SkyTrain slowed and the light rising above the church came into view from the high platform station, fleeting moments of nostalgia and longing of what could be quickly gave way to what was her life, of what she had become. It revealed the truth of her world that others getting off the train at the station would never know. She would end up looking away, waiting for the train to begin moving again, only to circle Burnaby and bring her back downtown to her home where the archer's bow condemned her and where Luc would be waiting.

But tonight she had no choice. Another voice forced her to get off at Joyce-Collingwood. The sting of Luc's words was muted by the cry that brought Magda to her feet. She was pulled along with the commuters eagerly leaving behind their work roles and obligations, shutting out the Luc's of their lives who also demanded more from them. The commuters could see the same light of the neighbourhood coming into view, filtering through the dreary rainy night. It didn't condemn, but reminded them why they laboured, and for whom.

Like Magda, they were weary, lulled by the rocking motion of the train on their ride home from work. Those fortunate to get a seat on the train could fall asleep but something instinctively aroused them at the precise moment they neared home. They would not circle the SkyTrain line indefinitely. There was family waiting for them.

Tonight the train brought Magda to a different point, awakening a voice from her past, providing her just one brief window to escape the pain that she tried to numb with drugs. She struggled with her free arm down the station platform steps to the street below and into the cold rain. The arched row of lit church panes was clearly in view just up Joyce Street, past Crowley Drive. Other commuters hurriedly walked past her, oblivious to her need. She remained hidden, shrouded in rain and darkness until she pushed open the large door after the others went in, wincing as she did so.

The doors to the church usually opened an hour before Mass. During Lent on Friday evenings you could also count on a handful of parishioners arriving early for confession, carrying umbrellas under the cold spring rain, engaged in a final moral checklist as they walked from their nearby cars. Rain in Vancouver had a particular way of turning one's thoughts inward, especially when low hanging mist blurred the transitional hours separating day from night. Umbrellas and upturned collars secluded people from having to talk with one another if they entered the church together, making the awkward shared space more bearable, especially for those who felt they telegraphed their sins.

Once inside, the contrast in surroundings to Magda's daily world was glaringly apparent. Like the plain concrete exterior, the inside of the church was also neither busy nor ornate. There was none of the frantic hustling and aggression she encountered every day at work. Only hushed tones among those gathered this evening. While it was different from the richly adorned church with colourful tapestries and icons her grandmother took her to as a child in the old country, the simple postmodern architectural design was surprisingly comforting to her. A lingering trace of candle smoke hung in the air, which Magda imagined rising above to the vaulted ceiling, through the four rows of arched windows that formed the elevated roofline, and up to Heaven above. What she imagined possible for ethereal smoke to penetrate was far easier than escaping the Downtown Eastside and Luc's grasp.

She could not stop shivering. Even though rain had not penetrated her clothes, she was perspiring with cold sweat. Her headache grew more intense. The fussing started again but she was not going to give in.

"Don't look at it. I can't."

Magda walked unsteadily towards a pew on the right side of the church, away from the early arrivers. She looked around nervously, hushing the baby she carried under her blue coat so its presence would not be known. Already today, Magda discovered that the quieter the baby was, the easier it was to pretend it didn't exist. The baby hardly made a sound on the SkyTrain.

Magda flinched again with new pain that she could not easily ignore, instinctively bouncing the baby in her arms to keep it quiet. She only saw two people in the confessional line along the wall on the other side of the church. Other parishioners started arriving for Mass and Magda feared they may sit close to her, or worse, go in line so she wouldn't have time before the moment was gone.

"God, hurry up," she muttered irritably to herself.

The baby started fussing. Magda jumped up to escape the sound, moving toward the entrance so she could leave if necessary. She was frantic now, thinking she had made a mistake coming here.

"Stop, just stop it will you?" she said with strained voice to the baby, angry for what had happened to her.

Magda made her way to a quiet alcove on the other side of the church that she failed to notice when she first came in, nearer the confessional. She wanted to ensure she would follow the woman next in line without having to get too close to her or anyone else. Already the woman looked twice as Magda approached. For Magda, she was used to such judgmental stares and expected no less in church. Despite these furtive looks, her corner sanctuary did not spare her the dove-like eyes of the statue of the Virgin Mary, in polished white stone erected upon a pedestal base against the side alcove wall where Magda stood. The statue's arms were held out to the side, welcoming, accepting.

Magda suddenly recalled the rosary her grandmother gave her when she was a little girl, before it all started. She remembered Babcia placing the beads in her hand, teaching her how to pray the rosary, smiling as she did so. Her grandmother's hand was wrinkled and bent arthritically but always warm. Always safe. But neither her grandmother's hand nor the rosary could protect her from the fate that awaited her. Both Babcia and the beads were gone now. Her grandmother died soon after, maybe from shame from what her son did. As far as the rosary, Magda either lost it or maybe later pawned it. She couldn't remember which. Like these painful memories, Magda could not endure the loving gaze of the statue, and looked away. Most days she avoided everyone's eyes, including her own reflection.

A man approached the alcove. Not unlike the men she knew from the street. Despite the statue's penetrating eyes and the accusatory looks of the woman near in line, his sheepish, awkward looks were familiar, giving her renewed courage. She was still in control and would not let him beat her, even though his kind degraded her many times before. She muffled the baby's cries with the small frayed blanket she took from the shared apartment, along with the small knife she needed, putting aside the memories once again to make her escape.

A green light above the confessional went on as a person exited, signaling it was time for the woman ahead of Magda to enter. To her relief, the approaching man continued to walk down the side aisle, past the confessional and statue. Walking by Magda was nothing more than a matter of habit. On the streets, unless people needed you for something, you were part of the facade of worn brick buildings that merely served as a backdrop as people hurried by with their busy lives. The inanimate statue, polished smooth by artisan hands and perhaps some parishioners' tears over the years ironically gathered more attention than the visitor and the child hidden under her cheap blue coat.

Meanwhile, the woman in the confessional reported her sins, as she did regularly at St. Benedict's every first Friday of the month. She was attractive, striking even, and confidently articulate. It takes some balanced creativity to recount the drama of your past month as she did, while at the same time rationalizing her behaviour towards people who had disappointed her. The parish social justice committee's recent outreach to the poor was a particular source of indignation. She hated seeing good money that she helped raise go to waste on those she felt chose to live irresponsibly.

"Like that woman who came in behind me," she thought.

She often reminded Father Bao through the mesh screen separating priest and penitent in the confessional booth whose contributions and political connections opened the pocket books of the rich and powerful to help build St. Benedict's, of which recent radical shifts in outreach philosophy were threatening to undermine. Long before he showed up, she helped build the community and was concerned of it now being diminished.

Still, she knew contrition was necessary and when to humbly ask for the Lord's forgiveness, taking to heart her penance, which she would dutifully complete through praying a decade of the rosary and whatever else she was assigned by the priest. She got up and left the confessional, stealing one more accusatory look at the stranger in blue waiting in line before returning to her pew.

Magda closed the confessional door behind her and was immediately aware of being enveloped in muted silence that magnified the sound of her own pounding heart and the baby's fussing, which grew more noticeable. She got down on the confessional kneeler, struggling to keep the baby cradled as she leaned on her other free arm. Beads of sweat dotted her brow.

"My, we are getting younger and younger for confession." Fr. Bao greeted Magda warmly through the darkened screen window, providing anonymity.

"I'm sorry, Father; I had to bring it with me."

"That's no cause for being sorry, my dear."

"I don't know about that, Father." Magda hesitated to say more, but abruptly stopped.

"You are only doing what you need to do for your baby, which is good."

"Is it, Father? So much of my life is about doing what I need to do to survive, which I'm not very proud of," she said bitterly.

"Is there something you have to confess? Our Lord is merciful and full of compassion," offered Fr. Bao patiently.

"I used to believe that."

"Then what belief brings you here tonight, if not the Lord's forgiveness?"

"I have to believe that there is someone or something I can still trust, when all around me I only know betrayal," Magda lamented, her voice still bitter.

"You can trust in the Church's sacrament of reconciliation to bring you some peace."

"I need more than peace, Father," Magda said sadly, her voice trailing away.

The baby fidgeted in her coat, cradled under her arm, and Magda paused to bring her out, shifting the baby to her other free side. She gasped audibly in pain.

"Are you okay?" Fr. Bao asked anxiously, the complacency that comes from hearing one too many self-righteous penitents like the woman before quickly erased from his mind. He wanted to be present to the woman on the other side of the mesh screen, reaching out to her like he did for some of the other women he knew.

Magda did not answer. She held her abdomen and felt the warm, wet flow between her legs. There was little room in the confessional to move around, but she managed to lean back on her calves and shift over a bit to leave room on the kneeler.

"Do you wish to continue at this time? It sounds like your baby needs your attention and you can come back. Is the baby's father with you?"

Fr. Bao long ago stopped making assumptions about people's marital status, even with those in his parish. There were enough of the regulars whose own children and grandchildren led eventful lives that made such assumptions risky. This was despite the equal risk of offending religious sensibilities in adopting more neutral sayings when the expected church nomenclature was reference to husband and wives, not partners. However, many of the regulars appreciated when he left them off the hook when asking about their children's better half, sparing their sheepish explanations.

"Oh, no, Father, they're not married," they would explain. He found such orchestrations wearisome.

Magda looked up abruptly at his question.

"I don't care to know the father," she shot back.

"Oh, I see."

"You see what? What do you know about me?" Magda hissed through darkened screen.

"You are correct, I don't know you. In this confessional, it is only the Lord who knows your heart."

The baby was crying now, as Magda distractedly replaced the blanket she had

around the infant, her own short gasps punctuating above the baby's cries.

"Are you sure you are okay?"

"Yes, I want to do this now. Please, let's get on with it."

"What's your name?"

"Magda."

"Magda, that's a really beautiful name."

"Can we start?"

"Alright, Magda," agreed Fr. Bao. He paused briefly, continuing with a formal voice.

"We begin in the name of the Father, the Son, and the Holy Spirit."

Magda awkwardly crossed herself with her opposite arm, trying to keep her balance on the kneeler with the baby at her side.

"I have had a tough life."

"Yes," the priest acknowledged compassionately.

"I am sorry for what I have done, lying and stealing and letting people use me to get drugs." She stopped, waiting for the usual judgment.

Silence.

She went on. "And I hate my parents, who were never there for me."

Fr. Bao stiffened at this, remembering his own past. Over time he got used to suppressing such memories so as not to get in the way of listening to other people's stories, often much more difficult than his own. He saved revisiting his own memories later when he was alone. He pushed the thoughts away.

"Yes, go on."

"That's it, Father."

"Okay," Fr. Bao offered slowly and evenly, careful not to imply more was required of her.

"Thanks, I have to get going." She started to push up on her free arm gingerly to help stand up.

"Do you wish to make an act of contrition before I offer you absolution?"

"What's that?"

"To tell Jesus in your own words that you are sorry for your sins."

Magda hesitated, uncertain, searching for words. Then, by rote, she recalled what Babcia taught her, which sounded hollow but strangely comforting.

"Oh, my God, I am sorry for having offended Thee, and I, I detest my sins, and, um... I firmly intend, with your help... not to sin again. Or something like that."

To Fr. Bao it sounded incongruous coming from the embittered woman he was speaking with a moment before, almost naïve and childlike.

Then her own voice returned and she added, "And forgive me what I have to do." Magda managed to stand up.

"I'm sorry?" Fr. Bao asked, confused.

"I have to go." She reached for the door and opened it. The light above the confessional turned from red to green, signaling the next person's turn. Blood seeped from Magda's leg.

"Wait, your absolution!" Magda teetered at the door, anxious to return to the nameless streets where she did have to remember or feel exposed as she did here tonight, in this church, in her state.

Fr. Bao did not delay, knowing she was about to leave, he quickly prayed the words of absolution:

"God, the Father of mercies, through the death and resurrection of his Son has reconciled the world to Himself, and sent the Holy Spirit among us for the forgiveness of sins; through the ministry of the Church may God give you pardon and peace, and I absolve you from your sins in the name of the Father, and the Son, and of the Holy Spirit."

"Amen."

The door clicked behind her. To complete the sacrament, he added perfunctorily to himself, "For your penance, pray ten Hail Mary's and one Our Father." Fr. Bao thought it was he who now sounded hollow.

The momentary silence of the confessional was soon broken by the next apparent penitent. Like Magda, this one was also unfamiliar with what an act of contrition was, let alone having the capacity to utter much more than a hungry, abandoned cry.

CHAPTER 2

The rain fell heavier downtown, washing litter from the sidewalks to the adjacent gutters and storm wells, some already clogged and overflowing. Momentary breaks in the downpour would provide a brief opportunity for people to dash from buildings to their parked cars or waiting cabs. Then the deluge would begin again as a new cell gathered force, scattering in its wake more debris of broken leaves, twigs and pine cones under the residential tree-lined streets and sidewalks around downtown.

People who laid claim to doorways as home drew their sleeping bags and card board box mats as close as possible under whatever overhang was available, turning over to sleep with their back to the street, seemingly oblivious to yet another rainy spring evening. Others more fortunate who lived nearby in upscale condo blocks could pull their drapes close and turn up lights and stereos if they wanted to insulate themselves from the sound of rain rapping on their ceiling high windows, so as not to dampen the mood in hosting a Friday night dinner party.

In Vancouver, most people go on with their lives despite the rain. It's a necessity really, given how much the city receives. Those who move to Vancouver find ways to embrace and dress for the weather, especially when remembering the comparatively colder climate from which most people came. It's not simply the rain to contend with, though, but the dullness of light. Like an airplane descending through continuous layers of cloud, it often doesn't break for weeks on end. Some people never adjust to this cataract-like effect pulled over their eyes and leave the city in despair, unable to cope with the persistent cloud and rain during the winter months. Those who stay and learn to thrive discover the city's many benefits.

Restaurants and bars do their part in helping instill the belief that rain is but a mere inconvenience that shouldn't stop anyone from going out and enjoying themselves. Use of warm colours and brightly decorative motifs encourage people to step inside. Umbrella stands guard the entrances of many establishments as if to symbolically require patrons to leave at the door any weariness of mind. The stands also ensure a practical recycled supply afterwards for anyone forgetting their umbrella once diners have had their fill of food and wine. Even the city workforce can be lulled by the rain. At least those sheltered inside away from the elements, enveloped by white noise as were Tanis and Sandy early that Friday evening. They sat opposite one another at metal desks in a red brick building below Cambie Street. The rain falling against their side of the department wall muffled Tanis' voice as she spoke on the phone while her male companion was absorbed in reviewing a police report. Tanis caught Sandy's attention only after she hung up. They never talked about the rain.

"You're going to like this one, Sandy. Our guys just got a call from a priest saying some woman left her baby at the church. Apparently, it was during confession."

Tanis anticipated her partner's sarcastic response with a grin, readying her own retort. Her partner looked up.

"What? Well, that's a first. Usually it's the affair resulting in a baby that brings people to confession."

"Maybe she was just leaving baby with the Father," she added dryly, pleased with her own quick wit.

Her smile dropped as she reviewed her scribbled notes from the first responders of the Vancouver Police Department on scene at the church.

Tanis was a veteran social worker serving as a community counselor on one of the Vancouver Police Department's Domestic Violence Response Teams in the downtown area. She had worked many complex cases involving abandoned kids and dysfunctional families, and knew encouraging Sandy any further with irrelevant commentary would not help their investigation.

Sandy's policing background and sense of right and wrong did not instill the same capacity for nuance as Tanis possessed. His indignation over people taking advantage of others had impaired his perspective on a few occasions. Still, Tanis appreciated Sandy's energy, which in recent months helped her stay engaged in their case work. Her partner's commitment kept her from feeling guilty that she had stopped caring on a personal level long ago. Sandy was passionate, principled and did not, as he described himself, "suffer fools gladly." Despite being only of average size and build, and impeccably clean shaven with fair hair, it was his intensity that could make his presence so intimidating, especially if he felt people were obstructing their investigation.

He was her proxy for believing the world could be a better place when all the horrific cases she had been involved with had a cumulative numbing effect on her. At this point in her career, she was just trying to secure her pensionable earnings. She was professional enough to do her job with integrity, without expending all her available limited energy just to move a case forward. She knew there would only be another case waiting for them anyways.

She lived alone in the downtown Wall Centre district where there was a commingling of tourists, business people and residential tenants to blend in without having to get involved with anyone. Sandy smelled stale wine on her breath some mornings, but surprisingly, not when he would have expected it. Say, for example, when they just investigated a tough abuse case that would keep him awake most of the night, requiring a drink or two to sleep in hope of blocking out haunting images from work. One image especially was hard to forget.

Sandy spoke of it to Tanis just once. Before Sandy was promoted to detective and began work in the domestic violence unit, he and his partner investigated a complaint at a dilapidated downtown apartment building of a strong odour coming from a neighbour's suite. They knocked on the door repeatedly with no response. Only after they heard a small child's faint cry did they gain forcible entry based on reasonable grounds. It wasn't the smell that overwhelmed them once the door was open, but the sight of a severely emaciated toddler alone on the floor, next to the couch where his mother lay dead from a heroin overdose. He was huddled there in the dark with sunken eyes, rocking against the couch with his blanket pulled close to his head.

The coroner estimated the woman died a few days earlier, and all during that time no one responded to the toddler's cries. No one checked in on them or even cared. It was only when the smell of her decaying body became so offensive that people bothered to call police to complain. The toddler just kept rocking and whimpered to console himself. Sandy picked him up and carried him to the ambulance, holding the boy all the way to the hospital. He died the next day from dehydration and severe malnutrition.

He told Tanis that it was this case that pushed him to become a detective and join the unit. He wanted to protect other children from similar fates. Realistically, he knew it wasn't always possible, but the memory of the boy's hollow eyes boring into him demanded he try. It took his own children's eyes to remember what was still possible; what childhood should be like.

For all his sense of passion at the injustice in the world, he and Tanis did not always share the same sympathy for their drug-addicted guardians. In retelling the case to Tanis, he barely mentioned the mother on the couch, who no doubt also suffered in her life. When he did comment about drug abusers, it was always with a judgmental tone. She often wondered if his real motivation was as much to punish the abusers as it was to protect the vulnerable.

Tanis felt Sandy resented her being assigned to him, as if her presence was intended to round out his learning or sensitize him. She found it ironic given that she was increasingly detached emotionally. She was able to feign compassion just by asking a lot of clinical questions based on her masters prepared social worker training, questions that were not always automatic for Sandy to ask during their investigations. If they were apparent, he didn't care to know. Like Sandy, she avoided certain questions. She seldom talked about what she did outside of work. All he knew was she visited her dad a lot. To be honest, he didn't know a lot about her. They both seemed to prefer it that way.

"When?" Sandy asked.

"About an hour ago, at St. Benedict's in southeast Van. On Joyce and Euclid."

"Is the baby okay?" he asked, concern rising in his voice.

"Yes, they brought the baby to Children's and Women's for assessment. Not sure about the alleged mom though. Priest said there was blood in the confessional and elsewhere in the church. First responders are there and other units are out looking for her. Not much description to go on. Parishioners who saw her stated they've never seen her before."

"What's the priest said?" pressed Sandy.

"I thought good Catholics like you know about the seal of confession, or whatever they call it."

Tanis was agnostic but curious about many religious traditions and would at times ask Sandy to explain the unique elements of his faith. They had many strained discussions about contraception, for one. He put forward the church's position as he had been taught, but his own lived experience was a contradiction that he could not reconcile with the teachings of his faith. This is where his capacity for nuanced reasoning was especially lacking.

Sandy didn't immediately respond. He was already annoyed with his wife's repeated arguments about women in the church and he didn't want to go there now. He felt lonely having to take his two kids to church by himself. At first, it was about giving Mommy a chance to sleep in and to have some alone time, but eventually it became a habit that his wife Allison never relented, which, like a lot of things in their marriage, Sandy reluctantly accepted. Like Tanis, there were unresolved areas in his life he was resigned to without wanting to defend himself.

Tanis dropped her smile again, seeing Sandy was irritated.

"Well, this is my case and I will be the one who decides who can say what or not," Sandy declared, with a bit more force than he intended.

He added, "What's the priest's name?"

Referring to her notes, Tanis replied, "Father Bao Luong. Vietnamese priest. He's at the rectory next door."

"Alright, let's go. And since when did you know it's called a rectory?"

"I read. And I watch old movies," she admitted.

They took their own cars, assuming they wouldn't be working all night and could leave separately for home afterwards. Both were on call the entire weekend so they decided to stay late at the department on Friday, preparing for their court appearances the following week and eating takeout food for supper when the call came in. Sandy got to the church first around a quarter to eight and took control of the investigation. Once Tanis arrived, they did a walk-through with the first responders who secured the area, verifying the known facts of the case. A forensic expert was brought in to take photographs, lift prints on the door of the confessional, and gather blood samples left behind.

While the other officers finished the witness statements, Sandy and Tanis walked across the church parking lot for the rectory. The rain continued to fall, splattering back at them as they stepped around puddles up the sidewalk to the priests' residence.

"Fr. Luong? I'm Detective Kohler with the Domestic Violence and Criminal Harassment Unit at the VPD, and this is my associate, Community Counselor Lyons. Do you have a few minutes to answer some questions?"

"Yes, of course," said Fr. Bao. He had a slight accent but spoke confidently and warmly.

He held the door to the rectory open for Sandy and Tanis to enter. The rectory was small with an open foyer adjacent to the living room, so visitors were immediately drawn into the priests' personal quarters. Tanis quickly took in the space, noticing the religious art, the bookshelves, but also a recliner chair and couch with a TV. She was suddenly embarrassed for thinking clergy didn't watch television.

Fr. Bao motioned for Sandy and Tanis to sit down but Sandy declined. They continued to stand in the entrance way, water dripping from their coats.

"No thanks, this won't take long. I know you already talked to the other officers, and they briefed us."

"How can I help?"

Sandy's voice had that inpatient edge to it tonight that Tanis recognized, meaning it was not a good time to interrupt his line of questioning. They had been domestic violence partners for about five months now, and were still learning to work together without occasionally acting at cross purposes or failing to pick up the other's instincts. She had her own social work and hospital contacts, which helped many of their investigations, but she recognized that as the detective of the team, it was ultimately Sandy's call what approach they took. She often felt tense around him but avoided confrontation if she could help it. She really didn't care if their relationship was good or not as long as the work got done.

"I know you will be limited in saying what you heard or saw, but is there anything that may be able to help us locate the woman that witnesses saw leaving the confessional to establish the baby's parentage?" Sandy glanced at Tanis after he said this.

"Just what I told the other officers," Fr. Bao offered, "that after the last person left I heard a baby alone in the confessional."

"The one the woman brought with her for confession?" pressed Sandy.

"I can't say if it was a woman or a man, or what was said," he said as a matter-of-fact.

"I know, I know," Sandy said dismissively, annoyed with the answer even after trying to set up the question for the priest from information drawn from witnesses.

He tried again. "So what did you see when you went in the public door to the confessional?"

"The baby with a small blanket loosely wrapped around it. A girl. And some blood. The blood is also in the church, along the side pews near the back."

"Yes," Sandy acknowledged, "and one of the officers saw blood in one of the pews."

"Really? Is there a lot?" Fr. Bao immediately felt embarrassed asking that, and then clarified.

"What I mean is, do you know if the woman people saw leaving is okay?"

"That's what we have to find out, Father, but first we need to find her and establish whether she abandoned her own baby, or abducted and abandoned someone else's. Either way, it's a serious matter."

"Yes," Fr. Bao answered, growing impatient with the circular questions and talking around the obvious, wary of being caught in divulging anything he couldn't.

"That's why I called the police right away. One of the parishioners held the baby until police and paramedics came and then took the baby away."

Sandy nodded.

Tanis looked on expectedly at her partner, sensing Sandy was going to try another tactic. Maybe they were beginning to jell as a functioning team after all, she thought.

"Father, since the baby obviously was not there for you to hear her confession, what can you tell me about her? Have you seen her before, I mean, recognize the blanket in which she was wrapped? Her cry even? Could you have seen the mother and baby at Mass another time, or baptized the infant recently?"

"I definitely didn't baptize the baby, as we only have baptisms in groups every other month and I heard the officer say the baby was a newborn. Mrs. Morrisey, the parishioner who held the baby when I called the police, also said it had to be a newborn. She said you could even smell that she was new."

Sandy looked at Tanis and nodded while continuing to write on the notepad she carried.

"Did anyone else in the church recognize the baby? I know evening Mass was cancelled but people were still there."

Fr. Bao didn't respond.

"Father?"

"Just what Mrs. Morrisey told me. I was just involved with calling the police and then giving information to the officers when they got here. They arrived within minutes, and the ambulance right after. Impressive, really."

"Right. And nothing remarkable about the baby that you saw?"

"Officer, I'm a celibate Catholic priest. You're asking the wrong person to give baby details," he said, smiling. "I hear parents telling me all the wonderful features of their children that they are obviously enthralled with, but basically it just goes in one ear and out the other. I have enough trouble not getting their names mixed up when doing baptisms, or remembering who the parents are versus the godparents. I've botched a few liturgies, I'm afraid."

"Fair enough, Father. That's all we need. If there is anything else you can think of, please contact us directly at this number. Any time."

Sandy handed Fr. Bao a card he pulled from his wallet. Tanis kept her gaze on the priest, noticing the crows' feet at the corner of his eyes on his otherwise youthful face, as well as seeing his thin dark hair falling forward to the side as he reached down from the foyer step for the card. She imagined how this man would have sounded if she turned to him in need in a confessional, if he would understand the burden she carried. He seemed so poised and collected, yet sad. Maybe sad like her.

"I will. And I will pray both mother and her baby are safe."

Tanis frowned imperceptibly.

"I thought you couldn't say if it was a woman whose baby you saw in the confessional?" Sandy quickly added.

Without missing a beat, Fr. Bao stated, "I didn't. But surely, this baby has a mother somewhere."

"Oh, don't be surprised, Father. There are a lot of people who hardly qualify as parents. Trust me," he said cynically.

Fr. Bao sighed heavily when they left, closing the door behind them. He was surprised at his own words. Yes, every person has a mother somewhere, he reminded himself.

He went to the kitchen and plugged in the kettle to make a cup of tea. He glanced at the clock, then the calendar on the fridge, noting his next day off. He thought of another person, remembering her voice and the promises he made to her. The phone in the living room rang, interrupting the brief silence in the rectory. He turned off the kettle before hurrying into the living room, glancing down at the call display. He was too preoccupied with his thoughts to react in time before lifting the receiver.

"Hello?"

"Fr. Luong?"

"Yes, speaking."

"This is Nargis Lekhar with CBC Radio. I understand you had some excitement at the parish this evening. Can you tell me what happened?"

"Oh, I'm sorry. Who am I speaking with?"

"690 AM. Was it you who found the baby?"

"I'm afraid I can't comment. I think it's preferable you contact the police authorities, who are dealing with this matter."

"So, you can confirm an unattended baby was left at St. Benedict's Church this evening?" the reporter pressed.

"I am not confirming or denying anything," Fr. Bao replied flatly.

"Father, this is a human interest story and your public statements can help locate the baby's mother."

"My comments, without intending, could actually harm the police investigation."

He added quickly, "Again, I'm sorry. But if you have any further inquiries, please contact our Archdiocesan Public Relations office. Thank you."

He hung up and put the phone on call forward.

"Great, now it starts," he muttered to himself. He was about to call his friend at the Archdiocese, knowing Ryan would give him shit for not calling earlier, when the doorbell rang. Annoyed, Fr. Bao went to the door, prepared to tell the person to go away. He was surprised to see Sandy again at the door.

"Detective?"

"I forget to tell you, Father, that the media will want a sound bite from you, so be careful what you say."

"I'm a step ahead of you. They just called. I gave them nothing. I will work with our communications person with the Archdiocese to issue a statement tomorrow, which I'm sure he will want to run by you guys."

"Thanks, Father, for your cooperation. Sorry to trouble you with all this."

"Can you tell the other officers to let me know when they are done with their investigation in the church so I can lock up? I will be up for a while. Don't imagine I will be going to bed early."

"Sure thing, Father."

"And can you do me another favour?" asked Fr. Bao.

Without waiting for a response, the priest said, "Can you stop any reporters from coming to the door?"

"We can for a little while, this evening anyways. They are a wily bunch so you have to expect some of them get through."

Sandy went to turn, adding with a small smile, "But as a practicing Catholic myself, Father, I suspect you will have your own share of questions to field from your parishioners. You might want to think about what you want to say before weekend Mass with your communications person, too."

"That's good advice," thought Fr. Bao.

CHAPTER 3

Fr. Bao closed the door, shutting out the chatter of police radios in the church parking lot. He was grateful his assistant was away this weekend, despite leaving him alone to do all the Saturday evening and Sunday morning liturgies. He wasn't that much older than his current assistant, Fr. Andrew Spivak, but the Archbishop felt Fr. Bao would be ideal to pastor this increasingly diverse parish community in East Vancouver when he appointed him two years ago. Along with his vision and pastoral sensitivity, Fr. Bao brought a maturity that exceeded his years. Unfortunately, such gifts were not equally recognized in the community.

Perhaps it was because his detractors always questioned his youth, or maybe because he frequently experienced resistance in moving certain initiatives forward in the parish that he recognized his emotional limits. He was too tired to give much more thought to what transpired tonight, deciding he would call Ryan in the morning. He trusted the police would run a little interference for him and his voice message machine would handle the rest. Thankfully, his cell phone was already off, having forgot to charge it the night before.

Fr. Bao remembered the Canucks were playing at home tonight and put on the TV to catch what was left of the hockey game. He looked forward to going to a game later this month with one of his physician friends. There was nothing like seeing a game in person, especially going with Tom, who had seats close to ice level on the blue line. Field hockey was popular in his native Vietnam but it was not until he immigrated to Canada that he really got to know, and now love, professional hockey. He imagined what an ice keeper in Ho Chi Minh City would be up against given the sweltering heat that he since grew unaccustomed to living in Vancouver.

He smiled to himself at the thought of trying to maintain smooth ice in Vietnam, and what rural villagers would think of the odd looking vehicle circling the ice between periods. Or, even more amusing, what it would be like for children playing in the snow dumped by the strange Zamboni outside the arena.

He had forgotten his tea and by now his cup and the kettle had cooled, so he poured a little Scotch, a gift of another parishioner who shared his pleasure for a good single malt, especially for occasions like this. It felt good to relax and be real, without having to worry about parishioners defining what his life should be like, and how he ought to lead the community. Friends like Tom and Ryan helped deflect the expectations others placed on him, who themselves dealt with their share of demanding public in their own jobs. Occasionally, the three of them went to games together, which was always a great evening out, whether the Canucks won or not.

The game wasn't very interesting and it looked like the Canucks were going to lose tonight, down four-one late in the second period. Without friends, it was harder to concentrate on the action taking place on the ice, especially watching it on TV. His thoughts instead drifted lazily back to being a kid again, free of responsibilities and others' expectations. He imagined Vietnam, viewing his childhood memories through the lens of his current life. Like encountering snow for the first time, not as he actually did in Winnipeg when he first arrived in Canada on a cold February afternoon after the connecting flight from Toronto, but experiencing the pleasure of snow as if falling under the heat of a South Vietnamese sky. For when the sun was hot and the humidity oppressive during the summer months in Vietnam, as oppressive as his life seemed of late given mounting conflict in the parish, how refreshing the falling snow would be. Even better, lying in the cool, wet leftover slush piled up outside an arena.

He imagined playing in it, joined by his friend Dat, who no doubt would be the first to discover how to make a snowball, and then master the art of throwing it, and in short order hit Bao in the head. Retaliating, little Bao, with his weak throwing arm, would miss Dat altogether. Dat always had the upper hand in things they did together.

"Dat Tan" he said out loud.

The flood of fond memories of Fr. Bao's childhood friend warmed him, much as the single malt warmed his throat on this cool, dreary Vancouver night. The rain was a little lighter in East Vancouver but still provided a mesmerizing presence as it fell evenly on the rectory roof. Fr. Bao drifted further in his thoughts, staring absently at the TV. Mechanically, he followed the end-to-end play of the hockey game with weighted eyes, while a cascade of memories unfolded successively with each team's rush up the ice.

"When did I last see him? In '78, or was it '79?" he thought to himself.

"It was already a few years after the war. My God, we were young. Just eight years old and full of adventure," he mused, smiling.

"It was always a game with us."

Fr. Bao took another sip before leaning back in the chair, his thoughts flashing disjointedly, thick and heavy in imagery. It was if he was in conversation with another in the room. Maybe too many such lonely conversations of late.

"I can still see Dat's face that night. His own excitement and fear, like my own. Both of us breathing shallowly. The hushed voices as we cut through the jungle from the road after hiding the small bus. The strangers whom my mother and the other villagers negotiated with. Then the sound of the surf on the beach that we came upon. Running under cover of a moonless night with Dat Tan across the wet sand. My mom and my sister holding hands, too. Leaving in those rickety boats being pushed out on the South China Sea. Then quietly paddling out in our little boats to reach the big boat past the reef, careful to not make a sound with our paddles. Being very, very still, Dat and me. It was an adventure."

His smile dissipated as staccato images of sights and smells brought him further back to the sea, and closer to the place he did not want to go.

"When we got into the big boat... God, how it stunk. Probably a mixture of dead fish and human waste. But it was the rolling sea and spray of surf that I feel still from that night. Crouching low under the gunwales and my spirit soaring as I tasted freedom that I had never known. My older sister was scared but I couldn't understand why she didn't enjoy the game like Dat and me. Our mother was stoic. No smiles from her, either. Soon I would understand."

"First, it was the waves when we were far out from shore and the light of day revealed how alone and small we were on the sea. It was like Dat made a huge snowball and hit me in the pit of my gut, jarring me from my childhood innocence as to what was really happening to us. Like the imaginary snowball fight, this game wasn't fun anymore, like all our games turned out when Dat got the best of me."

"Then it was the nausea and vomiting by people in the boat, and the crying from the woman when the old man died. They put him overboard without his clothes and shoes. That was the first dead body I ever remember seeing, and soon there would be more, many more. The cold of another two nights at sea came next, and always the hunger and thirst. The emptiness in my stomach mirrored the vastness of sea and sky all around."

"At least tonight my parched throat is quenched by the few sips of Scotch, helping to numb the flood of raw memories. I don't have to be the responsible priest and adult tonight. I can drift with the sea. The alcohol helps make the waves smooth and calm. The weight of the boat does all the work, letting me ride with the current without fear of capsizing."

"I remember the game became fun again when we saw land and my mother said it was a safe country. I sat up in front of the boat as the bow rose with the waves drawing nearer to shore, crashing down, sending the spray of sea over my head. I looked at my sister in expectant glee, but this game didn't last long, either. Angry people wouldn't let us get out. We had to give them things that we took from our house before we left in the boats, which we had kept hidden. The jewelry, especially. Some of the villagers in the boat swallowed their jewelry when the angry people weren't looking, which seemed so absurd."

"They had guns and pointed them at us, making us go back to sea. More crying and shouting. But the mean people couldn't be so bad because they gave us some food and water that lasted until the next day, at least for my sister and me and the other kids. It was just my mother and us in the boat with Dat and the other villagers. Dad died in the war defending the airfield at Khe Sanh and I don't remember him. Not even fatigue or disarming drink has ever unhinged memories of my father, for good or for bad. It was always just the three of us."

"The next day people were fighting on our boat and yelling at each other. Growing impatient. Becoming desperate. Now I was scared and no longer smiled. I was like my sister. She hugged me tight and gave me something to hold onto. Our mother was being pushed by some of the other people on the boat, not the ones from our village but the other villagers. People I didn't trust even though I didn't have words for it at the time. Finally we saw land again but it was small, an island maybe. And other boats coming at us, driving us to land. Really bad people with guns and toothless grins. Pirates. They made us land our boats and they shot one of our villagers when he tried stopping the bad people from taking one of the women. Screaming and panic and confusion. They took my mother and my sister and me and made us get out. My mother pleaded with them and they hit her. I didn't understand. I was terrified. She told me not to be scared and be brave like a man. She told me my name meant 'storm' and that I was strong and noble, and the storm in my heart would conquer the hurt."

Fr. Bao continued to muse as if telling the reporter who called him earlier what happened, not at St. Benedict's tonight, but all the events that led him to this moment in his life. The story he could not let go.

"She lifted me up and put me in the boat with one of the villagers and I thought we were finally able to leave together. The bad people took my sister and my mother to the jungle where people were screaming but the old man held me tight and wouldn't let me go run after them. More shooting and screaming. And the bad people pushed us out to sea while laughing at us with their bare gums, without my mother and sister and some of the other women. Just the older villagers and Dat and me."

"I never laughed or smiled on that boat again, even after we landed in Indonesia a few days later and were able to stay in a camp. We lived there a long time and people tried to cheer me up but I could only hold onto what my mother told me, to be brave like a man, to conquer the storm, which I learnt meant I could not play games or laugh anymore. Dat seemed to be able to play and go on but I knew he was different; tougher, meaner, and he laughed like the toothless pirates. We fought often and one day he stole my pants and pissed on me when he pushed me down. I did not let anyone see me cry, which I did only at night when it was quiet and I could hear the surf in the distance, and thought of my family."

"The camp stunk and there were rules and barbed wire and I wished I was back in Vietnam where I could play like I used to with the old Dat. Even if he threw a snowball at me, it would not really hurt and we would know it was just a fun game. It would be refreshingly cool under a hot sun. And we could still laugh. Finally, Dat left one day with his grandparents and younger sister and brother and I never saw him again. But the Dat I knew and loved left long ago anyways, before the internment camp."

"I heard from someone else in the camp that he went to live in the United States. But I didn't really care. I wanted to know where my mother and sister were. The only thing I ever heard was from someone whose boat also drifted too close to the men who roamed the seas, who later escaped from the pirate camps. He told us they killed the older women when they got sick or they just didn't want them anymore, or cared to feed them, but the younger girls they kept or sold, some to people in Thailand."

"One day I was moved to a smaller camp with the other kids, and nice women visited us. They were dressed funny but said they would work hard to have us live with them in Indonesia. They were Dominican Sisters and when their promise came true they made sure I learned to speak and read English, and ate well. Lots of government people visited us at the orphanage over the year, petitioning to find us permanent homes and reunite us with our families. They understood why I sobbed and ran upstairs to my cot in the dorm room when they told me I was going to be adopted by a family in Canada. Despite all their effort, they couldn't find my mother and sister. They allowed me to be sad and think of the family I lost, even though my adoptive family in rural Manitoba has always been good to me, lavishing me with their love and support as their only child without ever trying to replace my mother and sister or stand in the way of my searching for them."

"I know how hard the Sisters tried to find out information from the various embassy representatives, sending it to me in Somerset, and later in Vancouver, but we never located my mother and sister. The people told the Sisters, and me when I wrote when I was older, that it was best to forget about them. But I can never forget about my family. My own sister promised me she would come back. She told me this when I was put on the boat and pushed back to sea, without her or my mother."

Fr. Bao sat up straighter in the chair, taking another sip of Scotch. Clearing his throat. Leaning back again, heavily.

"On nights like this, when I am tired and strong drink numbs me, I remember my promise after searching for them in Thailand before going into the seminary that I should stop torturing myself and move on. I cannot accept that for all these years my mother and sister were in slavery or impoverishment, so better to think of them as dead, consoled at least by the memory of our lives together. It is easier this way. Besides, I have Michelle and André, who have given me roots, made me feel like I belong, and believed in me. I know they are older now and we only visit a couple times a year in Kelowna where they are retired. I am so grateful to my adoptive parents."

"But is this right?" Fr. Bao told the imaginary reporter. "Am I not also grateful for my first family? Am I abandoning their memory like the woman in my confessional did tonight? My mother also pushed me away, like Moses in the boat to save me, wanting me to go on and fight and forget about them and my pain. What motivated Magda to give up her baby if not a desire to spare the child of her mother's fate, and ironically, as I again find myself remembering tonight, my own unrelenting torture?"

Fr. Bao jerked as the announcer celebrated a third period Canucks' goal, probably too late to change the outcome in the game. Just like he thought it was too late to change what happened to him and his family. Getting up from the chair, he turned off the TV and grabbed his coat. He made his way outside to the church in hopes the police were ready to leave so he could lock up and go to bed. To close the door on the past for good just like he thought Magda closed the door on her baby and walked away.

Still, despite his intentions, he could not stop wondering how Magda could leave her newborn as his mother and sister left him on the beach. At least he had memories of a life together with his mother and sister. But Magda's baby? What memories would she ever have?

He tried hard to be like the Sisters who taught him to forgive, but he couldn't. She didn't even stop for her penance.

CHAPTER 4

While Sandy went to speak with Fr. Bao and confer with the first responders again, Tanis contacted the admitting neonatologist at the BC Women's and Children's Hospital to get a status update on the infant, now identified officially as Baby Girl Doe. Upon first examination, the baby was dehydrated with sunken fontanelles, hypothermic and exhibiting a weak cry, but in the past hour she began to tolerate some fluids and stabilize. There was no evidence of bruising, tenderness, lacerations or other sign of physical abuse, the physician confirmed. He estimated the newborn to be no more than eight to ten hours old given the cheese-like vernix still on the baby's legs and feet.

Privacy legislation prevented the physician from saying much more, including disclosure of hospital records to determine if a patient matching the description provided by the parishioners had recently delivered at the Centre, St Paul's Hospital or any of the other hospitals in the Lower Mainland. She knew that on a Friday evening she probably would only get a hold of on-call social service agency staff involved in urgent crisis intervention, who wouldn't be able to provide much more information, either.

Government was committed to trying to locate the parents of abandoned infants but within the parameters of its own enacted legislation. If social workers were not already actively involved in the care of this mother or baby, their search for the parents would be limited to a passive newspaper advertisement.

"Okay, now what?" Sandy asked when Tanis briefed him on what she just learned. They stood inside at the entrance of the church.

"Not much. There is no point in us pursuing, at least tonight. And we probably can't charge her for abandonment or failing to provide for the necessities of life if she shows up seeing that she left the baby with the priest. The medical assessment indicated the baby wasn't harmed."

"Dumping a kid in a confessional isn't harm? Tanis, we've charged parents and apprehended kids for a lot less things."

"It would appear her intent was to leave the baby where it would be safe, then left. She was probably in no position to care for the child so did the next best thing."

"The best thing would be to leave the baby in a hospital or with an agency," pressed Sandy.

"What if she hid her pregnancy and didn't want to be known? There are some who think that assuring anonymity may reduce the number of unsafe abandonments."

"Anonymity is a moot point. If the kid died as a result of her actions we would be going after her full press."

"You presume she was making a willful choice to harm the child, and that she was in her right mind."

"Tanis, you know intent is only part of it. We have to consider the consequences of her actions regardless if she was thinking clearly or not. You can't ignore what she did, no matter what frame of mind she was in."

"You don't know her situation and..."

"Oh, come on, Tanis," said Sandy irritably. "How can a person leave a kid, even if they didn't intend it harm? What would have happened if the priest decided he's heard enough sin for one day and cuts off work early, and then someone finds the kid dead the next morning?"

"Well, they're out looking for her and will bring her in for questioning when she's found. We need to talk to her to find out for sure." She saw no point arguing with Sandy and escalating emotions.

They walked to the parking lot, pulling their collars up to shelter their necks from the rain. Tanis looked back at the church, the light from the stained glass windows penetrating through the mist. She thought immediately of her dad and the remnant of light that tried to escape the clouds of his mind. Her father, whom she could no longer reach. She paused reflectively, her head still turned back to the lit building, rain falling on her grey hair.

"Sandy, maybe I'm wrong. Maybe she was in her right mind after all, and knew exactly what she was doing."

Tanis paused.

"She came here on purpose, to a place, or, like a symbol of refuge... a sanctuary."

"Sanctuary? Don't be getting medieval on me, Tanis."

"Not the church offering refuge. Maybe she left the baby for *him*."

"The priest? They didn't say the kid looked Asian, did they? No, I don't think so."

"You have to keep an open mind, partner."

"And you have to go home," Sandy countered lightly.

"Yeah."

She opened her car door, hesitating before getting in.

"You know I was the first to criticize those baby boxes that started popping up all over Europe to provide a means for anonymous and safe abandonment. I used to think they perpetuated a throw-away society. You don't like your kid anymore and you just throw it in a box."

Sandy looked closely at her, curious as to where she was going.

"But how many of those parents would have left their kid in a baby drop if they couldn't do so anonymously? Especially those people we see who have history with social services or police and don't want anything to do with us."

Tanis got in her car before Sandy responded, her door ajar. He held his hand over his head in vain to block out some of the rain.

"Not much difference in my mind than leaving a baby in a dumpster or back alley," replied Sandy. "The kid is still going to be pretty messed up later in life when they'd realize they were dumped, with no trace of their parents. What's that going to do to your head?"

"At least those kids live to see another day to have a chance to figure that out. Not much to say for that baby found last year on the banks of the Fraser," she reminded him.

With that she nodded goodbye to Sandy, reached for the door and pulled it shut. As she drove out of the parking lot onto Euclid, she wondered what sanctuary was available to help escape her own emptiness.

For a moment, Sandy thought of going back to the church before the first responders and forensic expert left. No doubt Fr. Bao would be back soon to lock the doors, he thought, and maybe provide a chance to talk with him further. But the day was late and Tanis was right, there wasn't much more they could do tonight. The rain fell unceasingly, eliminating much choice around his options.

When it rained days on end in Vancouver, there was some relief with nightfall. The darkened sky did not feel as heavy with cloud and dreariness as during the day. At night, traffic and street lights provided the necessary illusion that the city could soldier on without ever seeing blue sky. Florescence is a cheap substitute for sunlight. It was definitely worse waking up to rain and driving in it all day. Working late in the evening, alone and isolated in the confines of his car under a rain spattered windshield gave Sandy a place to think, even feel.

He drove home the longer way, off the highway, delaying his commute through nearby Burnaby that St. Benedict's straddled with East Van to his home further east in Port Coquitlam. He knew he wouldn't make it home before the kids were in bed anyways, so why rush? They understood on one level that their dad was a special police officer and detective, meaning some nights Daddy wouldn't come home at all.

Allison long ago accepted this too, coming to depend on her husband working late some evenings to provide her space, especially when she had to pick up the kids after work and make supper. By the time the meal was over and dishes done, if done at all, and she got the kids cleaned up and ready for bed, the last thing she needed was to give more of herself by getting into an intense discussion with her husband, or being his sounding board. Sandy knew this as well, and even if he did come home before Allison was in bed, they would both tune out in front of the TV until the first was ready to retire. Or, if they went to bed together, they would quietly escape in the solitude of their own books. Sometimes if one was talkative, and more often than not it was Sandy, they had to remind each other that tonight especially they needed quiet, which was basically their mutually agreed upon marriage cue that meant to shut up.

The front lights were on but the rest of the house was dark when Sandy pulled into the driveway, save for one table lamp he could see through the window at the bottom of the hallway stairs. He was grateful that tonight he could slip anonymously from the safety of his car to his living room and not be found. He smiled to himself at the irony that Tanis tried to point out to him only an hour ago. He mechanically opened the fridge door in the kitchen and stared. The fridge light briefly illuminated the darkened room. Nothing really interested him except a glass of something cold and wet. Orange juice would work. He sipped from the jug, then grabbed an apple and made his way upstairs, biting off big chunks of apple noisily. He saw light from under their bedroom door and was glad Allison was still up, but was not ready to enter, especially since he was eating, which would really jar the meditative space she had laid claim to earlier this evening.

He looked out the window onto the front street below, admiring his lawn, seeing the moisture glistening through spider webs laced randomly among blades of grass, translucent under the front door lights. Thin beads of moisture running down the window glass turned his awareness inside again, towards the other bedroom doors from under which no light presently shone. He suddenly felt glad to be home, happy for his family, to protect them, wanting the best for them. As usual, Timmy slept sideways on his bed when Sandy peered in through his bedroom door, with his quilt entangled around his leg. It always amazed Allison and him that despite their efforts to tuck Timmy in and carefully arranging his pillows to help align him straight on the bed, their son could still transform his bed into a jungle of sheets and stuffed animals, books and toy cars, that he brought to bed with him.

"I don't know how you can stand that, Kid," whispered Sandy, bending down to kiss him, careful when exiting the room not to stub his foot on some toy, or worse, stepping on a piece of Lego.

His sister, Nicole, adopted a different nocturnal stance. Lying on her back, her favourite comfort blanket nestled under her chin along her neck, she always appeared more restful compared to her brother while she slept. Her room reflected her inner equanimity, too. She was two years younger than Timmy, but even as a four-year-old Sandy could project out into her life and imagine her growing into adulthood with a calm, secure demeanor. With Timmy, however, he shuddered at the thought of how he would channel his kinetic energy, hoping that he would grow out of it. But with Nicole it was all about savouring her sweetness for as long as it would last.

Sandy always checked on the kids in this order before he went to bed; Timmy first, then Nicole, perhaps because his son's restlessness was the most direct off-ramp from his own frenetic life when he came home from work. When Tanis and he got involved with traumatic cases involving children, it would be too jarring to see Nicole sleeping so innocently. Timmy had a warrior spirit about him and seeing him thrashing about in bed gave Sandy some comfort that he could take care of himself, even though he was a challenging six-year-old to live with most days. Now that he was in school, he could try out his leadership skills on his peers that he had honed along the way in bossing around his younger sister.

Sandy was enveloped in the still darkness of his daughter's room, able to hear his breathing above Nicole's own. The rain had started up again, pattering gently against her bedroom window, laced in feminine curtains that Allison had specially ordered when they redecorated her room last year. They got Nicole her own grown-up bed that a parent could actually cuddle next to a child when reading a bed-time story. Sandy approached her bed and sat down next to her, knowing he would never wake her even when he rubbed her brow, whispering in her ear, "Daddy loves you." Allison always got after Sandy about this routine, saying it disturbed her, which he denied even though his argument was partially flawed, given the occasional flinch of his daughter's shoulders. Secretly he didn't deny the truth that he did it for himself, wanting her to know in the depths of her sleep that he was there for her.

He sat there, listening, hugging the edge of her bed, aware that he had the left over apple core in his other hand. A brown, rotting apple core could be left in Timmy's room without standing out and it would be a toss-up whether father or son left it, but there could be no hiding the evidence in Nicole's room.

He concealed the sticky wetness in his fist as he stood up, making sure he wouldn't wipe it on her bed. In the darkness of the night, it was easy to conceal what he held tightly in his grasp until the opportunity presented itself to throw it away. It was different in public. When Sandy threw his biodegradable apple cores or banana peels from his car while no one was looking, he still had to appease his guilt by saying it was not the same as littering. Some bird or raccoon would eat his on-the-run breakfast leftover he told himself, or it would break down and eventually nurture the soil. But what do you do when such remnants could not be tossed aside? When what we hold tight in our grasp cannot be let go of, whether tortured memories or people with whom our lives are entangled? Earlier tonight, the baby's mother found a good spot, he gave her that credit.

Remembering the case stiffened his demeanor, hastening his leave of Nicole's room. He quietly closed her door in an effort to seal off such thoughts, in one final gesture to protect his children from what lay beyond childhood, at least for some kids. He tossed the apple core in the hallway bathroom waste basket, guided by the *101 Dalmatians* night-light that faithfully shone when little bladders commanded emptying. Funny, Sandy thought, how a polka-dot dog could assure his family that all was safe in their house. Pongo's light even pushed away Sandy's own dark thoughts. He wiped his sticky hand on the facecloth the kids used earlier this evening after brushing their teeth, and turned towards the master bedroom.

The rain spattered harder against the hallway window next to their door. Sandy reached for the knob, careful to turn it quietly. The light no longer shone under their door.

CHAPTER 5

The rain continued to fall heavily near downtown. Those waiting for the SkyTrain were sheltered under the platform canopy, but as the temperature fell steadily near midnight, it was no longer protection from the damp air that clutched at a person's bones. Especially when exhaustion after a long evening shift for weary commuters gave up the last bastion of protection from the penetrating damp. Relief at finally seeing the approaching light was quickly dampened by seeing what the train carried. The Canucks must have rallied late to force overtime, as there weren't usually a lot of hockey jerseys on the SkyTrain when Helena got off work, except during playoffs when there was always post-game parties on Robson Street, whether overtime or not.

Even before the train doors opened, Helena could hear the raucous noise of the revelers, mostly men, but it was only when the doors did slide open that you could actually feel the pitch of the crowd, fueled by beer and a disappointing loss. Helena did not understand hockey and couldn't care less if the crowd was in a happy or angry mood. She clutched her bag tightly and looked furtively for the nearest seat away from the revelers, many of whom stood, barely casting her a look. There were obviously other women more interesting to them among those who got on at the Main Street - Science World station. The SkyTrain jerked forward once the doors closed, with the crowd banter magnifying the roar of the train reverberating off the station walls.

Helena leaned into her seat as people moved about the train, trying at the same time to avoid any contact with the woman next to her. One person wearing a white Canucks home jersey yelled to another in blue, every sentence containing at least one "fucken-eh," or just plain "fucken." His compatriot's vocabulary was no less colourful. Home Jersey pulled at dark blue Away Jersey for added effect, punctuating his "fucken-eh" while motioning towards the young woman sitting next to Helena, purposely bumping against Helena as the train sashayed back and forth. Helena instinctively leaned inward, relying on the universal suspension of stranger contact rules when a common threat was sensed.

Annoyed and scared, she looked up quickly at Home Jersey, seeing something had changed. She looked again and saw his face had turned from overconfident mob leer to confusion, and then shame. Away Jersey must have seen it too, as he became quiet, noticing what was visible only if you stood nearly over the seated persons, as the compressed mob was required to do. Helena felt it then, understanding dawning as to what had already come to the now silent pair of Canucks jerseys. She looked to her right and saw that the woman in blue coat was ashen, barely noticeable through the long fallen straight brown hair that covered the side of her face. In her reflection in the SkyTrain window, she could see her mouth was ajar. Helena's scream barely pierced above the crowd. Her own beige coat took on the Canucks' vintage jersey orange as Magda's bright red blood seeped from her seat next to her and onto the floor below.

CHAPTER 6

Fr. Bao was up early Saturday in preparation for the parish committee's social justice retreat beginning with Mass at eight. Actually, it was an opportunity to sleep in as regular weekday liturgy started an hour earlier, and if he was going to exercise on his stationary bike beforehand, he generally had to get up by five. But he was tired this morning and, knowing he had a long day ahead of him, he decided to skip exercise altogether and instead enjoy an extra cup of coffee with the paper. It wasn't often that Fr. Andrew was away, allowing him the added freedom of the rectory, feeding his introvert self.

But there were other reasons that wearied Fr. Bao that day.

"These people drive me crazy," he muttered, tossing the paper he retrieved from the front mailbox on the kitchen table. He half glanced at the front page, not absorbing the headlines, distracted by what he would endure today.

"These professional Catholics are never happy with anything we do."

Thoughts of the Nichols consumed him and he rehearsed what he would say if they objected to the five-point parish plan he put on the agenda for discussion at the retreat today. He was still annoyed by last week's encounter with Stephen and Marie Nichols following Mass.

"Father, we have a question about your outreach ministry proposal. Marie pointed out something to me last night that we think you should seriously consider."

Stephen's presence was immense; a large man with an equally big voice. He was a formidable debater and unafraid of conflict.

"Meaning, accept unconditionally," thought Fr. Bao, as he looked blankly from one to the other.

"Probably best that you add it to the agenda on Saturday so everyone can benefit from your idea, Marie," Fr. Bao offered in a conciliatory tone.

He felt that Marie had a little more imagination for the reality of people's lives and the need for a pastoral approach when interpreting church teaching, so he was never quite sure whose voice Stephen spoke with. Marie had her own distinct take on things. Still, he didn't want to commit too soon until he saw what the Nichols had in mind. He never quite understood how both husband and wife were allowed to serve on the same parish committee; a decision he inherited when he came to St. Benedict's. He looked forward to when they would both rotate off next year.

"Certainly, Father," Marie agreed, but quickly added, "Maybe you should send this out in advance of the retreat. People always take more notice when it comes from the pastor, especially if you allow enough time for people to reflect on the proposal. You have a way of getting us to think."

There was earnestness to her tone that suggested she truly believed floating out an alternative proposal would enrich the conversation.

"I see. Why don't you send me a note with your proposal and I'll take a look at it."

"Oh, no need to bother you, Fr. Bao," interrupted Stephen. "We already talked with the others, who agree, so you can save a step and circulate it now."

Fr. Bao always imagined standing outside of such conversations as a detached observer, wondering at the exact moment when the manipulation began.

"Incredible," said his observer-self, hovering above their conversation. "And with complete lack of insight into how transparent they appear," he thought.

Fr. Bao paused before simply replying with a tone of mock disbelief, "Really?"

Not wanting to give them the satisfaction of falling for the trap of asking them to describe the proposal, he added, "Well, then I guess people are already aware of its potential merits, including any weaknesses or short sightings, as there always are with any good idea." It was Fr. Bao's own contribution to the game.

"Still, it's prudent I make a final determination as part of my chair responsibility once I have a chance to read it," he concluded evenly.

"Yes," Stephen agreed, and then continued, "And of course, too, I'm sure the Archbishop will be delighted to know this after we talked to him about it at the Family Life conference."

"He seemed interesting in learning more about it. I was surprised myself," Marie added.

"Ah, the Archbishop trump card," observed Fr. Bao's cynical voice from above. "I'm surprised they played that card so soon. Usually they wait awhile. Must be a bit anxious being it's their last year on the committee and they want to get everything in while they have a chance."

Fr. Bao had a great relationship with the Archbishop, believing his superior had his back. A wise and compassionate man, the Archbishop was good to redirect people to those whom they needed to be in direct conversation with so as not to undermine his priests' authority. Besides, he had his share of headaches from the other Stephen and Marie-type folks in his own ecclesiastical circles that he didn't need to encourage further escalation of issues to his office. He really took to heart the principle of resolving issues closest to the grass roots as possible, for which the clergy in his diocese widely respected him.

However, certain advocate groups were unrelenting in their pressure, accurately quoting doctrine or papal statements that couldn't be readily dismissed. How the Archbishop navigated some requests, Fr. Bao could only guess, but he had been privileged to get some unsolicited advice from the Archbishop in handling his own parish conflicts that required growing thicker skin.

41

"It never pays to make enemies, Father, but you need to know when to make a stand and push back."

That one consoling piece of feedback from the Archbishop was Fr. Bao's own secret trump card. Just knowing it was up his sleeve was enough without having to play it.

"I'm sure the Archbishop will indeed be pleased that we exercised due diligence in considering the strengths and weaknesses of all proposals in developing our social justice pastoral plan when he reviews our submitted report after the retreat."

Stephen grew red in the face while Marie's smile lessened a tad.

Before they could say anything, Fr. Bao directed, "Just send the proposal to Natalie in the office," and left for his rectory.

That was five days ago, after Tuesday evening Mass. The agenda came out late Thursday afternoon and thankfully, he didn't see the Nichols yesterday. His assistant had morning liturgy before leaving the city, and Fr. Bao was busy all day meeting with two families to plan funerals for early next week. He couldn't remember if the Nichols were there at church last night with all the commotion.

His private cell phone buzzed, startling him, bringing his awareness back to the paper he absently flipped through. He had plugged his cell in overnight but only turned it on after getting out of bed. Almost as soon as he heard Ryan Scott's voice in his ear, his eyes fell on the small story in the right hand corner of page three of *The Province*. The Archdiocesan spokesperson immediately asked, "Bao, did you see the news? I already got a couple calls from media for comment. Did they reach you?"

Fr. Bao listened as he skimmed the short story, describing the events of last night regarding a baby left at the parish and the ongoing investigation. Rather benign, he thought.

"It seems fairly straight forward, nothing more than what I acknowledged publicly last night. Ryan, I can't say more, you know that."

"I'm not talking about the story in the paper. It was obviously too late to run it when the paper went to print. It's the one on the radio." For a moment, Fr. Bao wondered how the Canucks game ended, as they were beginning to rally before he turned the TV off.

"They found a woman on the SkyTrain last night who sounds like she bled to death. They are linking her as the unidentified woman at the parish,

Bao. The media is going to want to talk to you. Are you okay if you let me issue comment on your behalf? I will restate our key messages. Nothing changes as far as our ability to confirm or deny the existence of a person you saw for confession, other than what parishioners disclosed to media last night about the baby and a woman in a blue coat leaving the parish."

"Oh no! You're kidding?" Fr. Bao felt light headed, trying to recall Magda's words to him last night. He remembered she was in pain and that he asked if he could help her. "Did I miss something that I just didn't hear?" he wondered. For what seemed like minutes, he stared at the small knick on the kitchen table next to his coffee cup, noticing every minute detail in the grain of wood and where the shine of the veneer was missing.

"Bao?"

"Yes, yes please. I have a social justice retreat all day and prefer you say I'm unavailable for comment."

"Right. The story may get legs and I can't say media won't push you to provide a statement. You don't have to and you're not being rude to say so."

Ryan had worked with Fr. Bao on another media story a few years back when vandals had desecrated parts of a nearby cemetery. It turned out to be a foolish act of vandalism by teens without racial or political motives, unlike the series of other headstone toppings and graffiti tagged synagogues previously in the city that year that were targeting Jews. He knew Fr. Bao was a principled man and would not get pulled into giving public comments that would not serve him, or the Archdiocese of Vancouver, well.

"I already saw online media comments by both pro-life and pro-choice groups weighing in. Surprising how people already have an opinion about someone's life before the facts are known. The police aren't saying much and neither should you."

"Suits me fine."

"But be prepared, Bao. You may have been the last person—allegedly the last person that is—to have talked to this woman. A baby was left in your parish, and although no one is claiming the baby, predictably two advocacy groups are both laying hold to this woman as their poster person for their respective cause."

Ryan stopped short. He had his own opinions about any groups that become so dogmatic that they fail to appreciate the complexities of individual cases. Of course, as an official representative of the Roman Catholic

Church he would always issue comment in support of the pro-life groups. He respected the Catholic Women's League and other mainline groups like the Knights of Columbus, but some individuals he had encountered over the years left him wondering if they were deeply wounded themselves and playing out their own family of origin issues.

"I mean, seriously," thought Ryan, "how did placards and website images of dismembered aborted fetuses not border on exploitation itself, and undermine the dignity of the unborn?"

He had many vociferous arguments with friends and sympathizes alike whether this awe and shock approach simply alienated people, and inadvertently thwarted their overall efforts to rally public support. Ryan worked in television before becoming Communications Director with the Archdiocese, and his editorial team frequently had to discern whether airing stories with images of violence or death was their journalistic responsibility as a matter of public interest without exploiting the dignity and privacy owed to victims and the families who mourned them. Even when disclaimers were included to warn viewers that some images may be disturbing, it was still a judgment call. Images of bodies strewn across a tarmac following a plane crash or violent altercations between rioters and police were newsworthy, and the public deserved to know what was really occurring in the world without censorship. But balanced reporting required some ethical sensitivity, he felt, to consider the needs of both the individual and the common good. Despite this commitment to ethical journalism, there were still occasionally some who accused the network for being sensationalistic, focused only on improving their ratings.

The last thing Ryan wanted to do was venture again into this polarized debate and be forced to take a side, or let Fr. Bao do so. Still, the Archdiocese would be asked for a comment and he wanted to be the architect of their own balanced position rather than having to react, especially if some fanatic forced their hand.

"Not to worry, Ryan. I have enough on my hands right now trying to rally support for our outreach ministry. As if opening a community soup kitchen at the Church will encourage homelessness and poverty!"

"So I hear. Good luck with that one, Bao. Seems no one wants the poor in their backyard."

"Especially if they leave their babies."

"You don't know she was poor, Bao. You'd be surprised at the number of women who hide their pregnancies, especially young girls who may come from very well-to-do homes." The journalist was coming out of Ryan. He remembered covering a story years ago about a rise in teen pregnancies and the options that girls faced, including unsafe abandonment in a back alley or dumpster. He wanted to inquire further to satisfy his own curiosity in what Bao saw but knew it would be inappropriate to push it.

"Anyways, Bao, not to worry. If you get called or approached by media, just redirect them to me. You can give them my work number. I'm forwarding all my calls to my cell phone this weekend."

"Does that offer include running interference at my retreat?" laughed Bao.

"Absolutely!" assured Ryan, and they both went silent knowing the inevitable conflict Bao faced week in and week out.

After saying goodbye, Fr. Bao looked outside the rectory to see if any media were gathering. Seeing none, he quickened his pace to get ready for the retreat, hoping to get over to the church before any showed up.

"I guess it's easier to deal with the enemy you know than one you don't, after all," he muttered flatly as he reached for the last sip from his coffee.

Looking in as Mass was being celebrated, no one would have thought anything was different. Only hours previously, the church crackled with police radios and the snapping of photographs. This morning the congregation sang as they always do, a little off key, and they kneeled and responded to prayers on cue. Good natured questions from parishioners before Mass like, "Wow, you sure had an interesting evening last night, eh, Father?" or, "That's got to be a first for St. Benedict's. How are you doing, Father?" were relatively easy to deflect with an equally noncommittal social pleasantry. He didn't even think of connecting the readings with the events of last night in his brief homily. He was actually quite grateful when he remembered only later in the day he had not drawn attention to the event during the service. The closest he came to consciously remembering was praying during the intentions for the success of the parish social justice committee retreat that day, asking for the Lord's wisdom to guide the committee's deliberations in serving the poor. A blanket prayer that pretty well covered everything, he thought.

He glanced occasionally at the Nichols, who sat in their usual section of the church, and the other committee members spread out among the fifty or so gathered for Saturday morning Mass. There were a few more than normal given the retreat. Fr. Bao was more preoccupied with the agenda and the inevitable confrontation with the Nichols, knowing that their formal request to pre-circulate their amendment with the agenda package was not honoured. He made that call almost immediately. There were some things in his administrative world he learned did not always require consensus.

CHAPTER 7

The care facility atrium was brightly adorned with the morning light that streamed through the high glass panel walls. The developers had renovated and modernized the older building to capture as much light in the atrium as possible. It helped offset those days, and sometimes weeks, when Vancouver was oppressed by constant rain and cloud. Those mornings when the sun shone the atrium was bathed in light dispelled the gloom Tanis often felt upon entering the building. The facility was straddled on either side by larger condo developments in downtown Vancouver, not far from Tanis's own building. She requested this facility because it was only a ten minute walk to visit her dad, at least that was the plan.

Over the past fourteen months, however, her dad's progressive dementia had made intelligible conversation with him nearly impossible. He was generally well-cared for but the staff could only do so much, and she never felt her dad ate properly if she wasn't there for at least one of the meals to feed him, often breakfast, and especially so when the atrium light beckoned.

She paused as she walked through the atrium. She normally walked very purposely, much as she was intentional about everything she did in her life. But she had noticed lately that she needed more time to collect herself before taking the stairs up to the second floor where her dad resided. The atrium communicated an atmosphere of light and life, obviously a signature feature reflecting a philosophy of holistic care in which the organization prided itself. There was a time when Tanis felt that spirit throughout the building, in the pervasive light of the atrium, in her dad's room and in the smiles and laughter of staff and other residents. But where had the light gone from her dad that filled her heart; the light she had always experienced in her relationship with him?

She was always very close to her dad and the pictures in his room that served as conversation pieces depicted the many shared moments of their lives. Tanis' favourite was the picture of them when he taught her to ride her bike at age four. They both have the same earnest look on their faces, Tanis looking down at her feet trying to master the art of pedaling, while her dad held one hand on the centre of the steering wheel. He was looking up to see where they were going while his other arm cradled her back, steadying her.

Her dad, Marvin, was a good man, looking after her mother when she was dying of cancer. She admired how he stood by her to the end, sacrificing so much of his own leisure time with his retirement friends, even giving up his golf membership to attend to her. He always seemed to be a man of two hands; one guiding his family, with the other supporting her mom and Tanis from falling.

Other pictures evoked similar stories of guiding presence. For example, the one when they were camping in the mountains; Marvin struggling to set up the tent while mom and daughter huddled near the fire taking pictures. He looked both frustrated and proud at the same time. And the one that invited the most comments by staff and visitors; the one with her mom, Audrey, while he washed her hair when she could no longer do so given painful lymphedema in her left arm. Unlike the mastery in which he taught Tanis to ride or in setting up shelter, he appeared so helpless in this picture as Audrey and Tanis laughed. Here it was Tanis who offered a hand to steer him in the art of setting a woman's hair, and Audrey who provided just enough encouraging laughter so as not to shame the poor guy.

Yet now, at eighty-three with no wife's hair to wash or child to watch over, with his body tiring, so did his mind. At first, his speech was garbled and he had difficulty finding words, but it was still relatively easy to follow along in the context of the conversation. Then there was no context. Marvin would speak randomly, at times seeming to want to make a statement, other times as if to pose a question. No sooner than he began, his voice stalled. Tanis saw how frustrated he became.

It was as if he gave up conversing all together. Either it wasn't worth the frustration or he sensed no one bothered to listen anymore. He became more a shell of his former self. Staff meticulously bathed and dressed him, even applying the Old Spice cologne that he once liked so that his familiar scent would linger in the air of the room when Tanis entered.

Approaching him to say hello, she wondered who this man was that she touched. He no longer looked up, often remaining stooped in his geriatric recliner.

"Hi, Dad!"

She drew closer to his ear.

"Dad? Morning, Dad. It's a beautiful day out."

The radiator floorboards ticked quietly as the steam expanded the hot metal, warming the room. Sunlight from across the hallway edged towards the doorway of Marvin's room, as if reaching out to say hello and warm up tired bodies. The chatter of health care aides could be heard down the hall over the incessant call bells. Someone obviously needed assistance off the commode.

Tanis felt her own helplessness, self-conscious about having another one way conversation that had become a frequent pattern of her visits.

"Oh look, Dad, let's see what you have for breakfast this morning," feigning excitement about what was no doubt the usual slightly soggy toast, an egg, a bowl of Cream of Wheat, and some lukewarm coffee. She lifted the lid of the food tray that had been placed on the table before him and stirred the milk and brown sugar in the Cream of Wheat, looking up to see if the aroma would have aroused her dad from his lethargy.

Nothing.

Marvin was on calorie count, taking in less and less each day. Several cans of food supplement were unopened on his bedside table. The clinical dietician had spoken with Tanis earlier in the week, indicating she was concerned about his weight loss. Although he still had a gag reflex and managed to take in food orally when alert, it was becoming more laboured. Like his speech, his body was beginning to declare that the benefit of eating was no longer worth the effort.

"Here Dad, try this." She blew gently on the spoonful of warm Cream of Wheat and brought it to his lips. He pursed spontaneously but not ajar enough to receive the food. Most of it spread over his upper lip.

"C'mon Dad, you need to eat. It's good. Try some."

"Dad?"

"Dad?"

The radiator ticked encouragingly. The sun's hands now stretched out beyond the hallway, further into Marvin's room.

"Dad!" The frustration in Tanis' voice startled even herself but guilt gave way to instant relief when Marvin lifted his head and opened vacant eyes towards her.

"Hi Dad, good morning," the soothing tone returning to her voice.

"How are you, Dad?"

He stared at her. She refused to do what she heard other family members telling their parents that it was so-and-so here. Even if her dad was totally unresponsive, she promised herself she would never greet him by saying, "It's me, Tanis."

She had to hold on that even unconsciously her dad recognized her voice, or there was nothing left. There was no point continuing on if all their memories of life shared together were cast aside into the oblivion of a vacant mind. She could not go there.

The glass of red wine helped keep such dreaded fears at bay when she was alone in the quiet of the evening hours in her condo, tired when a day's work lowered her guard.

Alone when she could have another one-way conversation.

She held another spoon to his lips, which this time he took in mechanically. She smiled when, after seemingly an eternity, he swallowed.

"See Dad? It's good. Here you go, open up." She hated herself for talking to him this way, as if a child. The impatience returned to her voice.

"Okay Dad, try some more." She lightly tapped his lips until they opened. She looked down at the tray, annoyed how long this would take at this rate.

He held the food in his mouth, coughing feebly. She knew he would swallow if she got fluid in him, a trick she quickly acquired since it became necessary to assist in his meals. She kept encouraging him while preparing his coffee, adding a little milk and sugar, taking a sip herself to check the temperature. His head drooped further. She reached for the syringe left in the cup by his table and drew up an ounce or two of coffee awkwardly and then squirted a bit in his mouth. Half leaked out the side of his mouth and he began coughing. She knew the meal was over for both of them.

Sandy's call on her cell phone was a welcome relief, which she stepped out into the hallway to take. Of course she would come in, and no, she wasn't busy, and yes, come pick her up at the care centre in thirty minutes.

"Hey Dad, that was work. I have to work today, even though it's Saturday. We have this case we're on. You remember Sandy, right? He's coming to get me now so I guess I have to go."

A health care aide peered in the room.

"Is he finished with his tray?"

"Yes, my Dad's finished." She slightly reddened.

The aide looked at what was left in the tray. "He didn't eat much. Should I leave him the coffee?"

Tanis became uncomfortably aware of talking over her dad. It was so easy to do that now, which she also hated herself for it.

"I don't know. What do you think, Dad? Should we leave your coffee? You might be thirsty later." The words sounded so disingenuous to her.

The aide knew this charade, and waited politely for the predictable reconsideration.

She said quietly in a half whisper, shaking her head, "I don't think so. You better take it all away."

The aide gathered up the contents while Tanis irrigated the syringe in a cup of water before returning it to what she hoped was still a relatively clean empty cup. It reminded her of how vulnerable she felt leaving her toothbrush in a cup by the sink when staying in hotels. She always wondered how clean those cups were, and if anyone ever bothered to replace them.

The aide left with the tray, marking the calorie count on the sheet posted on her dad's door. Tanis stood up from the side of the bed. She realized she had not taken off her coat.

"Dad, I'm leaving now. I have to go. I will be back later tonight or maybe tomorrow. I hope you have a good day. I love you."

She reached down to kiss him on his cheek, bristled with white whiskers that matched his sparse and balding head. It always reminded him as a young child playing on his lap, brushing up against a two-day beard on weekends. In her adult years, she only knew her dad as immaculately groomed and dressed. Very professional. Not like this.

"Bye Dad," she said again. She got up, and through tears in her eyes, she saw the marginal numbers on her dad's calorie count posted on the door for all to see that not even Tanis could no longer deny. She turned, following the rays that spread across the hallway towards the stairwell, with the red exit light above the door.

CHAPTER 8

Allison was up early and heard Sandy take the call from the bedroom while she towel-dried her hair in the en suite bathroom. She could tell it was work just from his tone of voice. At first she thought it was their friend Don calling, letting him know he had a tee-time booked. The rain had let up and sunshine was in the forecast, which was always a bonus in the Lower Mainland. She cut him some slack if part of his weekend included golf, as he was very good about his share of yard chores and commitments with the kids. When he did play a round, it was usually early enough that he was home for most of the afternoon, and would make sure the rest of the weekend was devoted to family. She knew the social aspect allowed him time to relax with friends and to get away from the incessant restless energy in cases, especially those investigations that spanned weeks at a time.

She was annoyed, already readying herself for the predictable let down of a day ruined. It was not the time at work that bothered her; sometimes it just meant Sandy following up on a lead for a few hours or getting a court order to search a premise. Rather, it was that he came home a cop, and it would be hours before the cop in him was laid aside. He may actually be away from the house longer golfing, and even irritable about how his game went, but he could bounce back quicker. When he sliced into the woods or missed putts, the sooner he forgot about his game the better. In which case, getting involved with things around the house or playing with the kids the rest of the afternoon helped.

But when it was work he would not want to forget, or could not. Outwardly, Allison saw he appeared the same, yet there was always a detachment about his presence around the home, even during love making after the kids had gone to bed, that left her feeling lonely. She was not the only passion in his life.

She had learned not to sulk at home, however. The unexpected phone call from Sandy's work was the signal for Allison to take the initiative and make alternative arrangements. She knew she couldn't count on Sandy's promises that he'd be right back, no matter how sincere his intentions. Timmy and Nicole sensed this too, although they had no words for it. Everyone just became a little more guarded, no doubt as a way of protection from disappointment, or worse, resentment.

Try as she did, it was not easy to hide her hurt feelings.

"I suppose that was work?" Allison asked, more as a statement than a question.

"Uh-huh." Sandy learned it only made it worse getting into explanations that she didn't want to hear anyway.

"When do you think you'll be back? I'd still like to go to the garden centre later today, and I can't get all the soil and peat moss stuff myself."

Sandy didn't answer the question. Instead he said, "I was in late last night. Did you hear the news?"

"About the baby at the church? I figured you and Tanis would be in the thick of that."

Sandy paused, deciding whether he should say anything else related to work. Thinking better of it, he said, "I shouldn't be too long."

"Uh-huh." It was Allison's turn to acknowledge out loud what they both knew would happen to their Saturday plans.

He grabbed his wallet from the dresser, looking way. Sandy turned, saying, "I need to go now but tell the kids I'll see them later."

54

He added defensively, "They're proud of my work helping women and children, you know."

"No one is saying we're not Sandy. Yes, they're very proud of their father. I'm proud of you, honey. It's just that we wish we would see that same call to service around the house," she offered gently, with a tone of vulnerability.

"I do lots of work around the house."

"You know what I mean, Sandy."

"Yeah, I know." "Do you?"

"Of course."

"We want you to be here with us."

"You mean you do." He smiled, relieved that this time, again, he got the needed support to leave without feeling guilty.

"The kids, but yes, me too. So try to get home early so we can get to Rona.

It's supposed to be nice today and I want to work in my garden. You said you'd help with cutting that tree out."

"God honey, if you'd have it your way I'd be cutting down trees for you every weekend."

"Well, you should have thought of that when we moved here." Allison smiled.

"Hurry then. I want to do hamburgers on the BBQ for supper. The kids have been asking all week for burgers."

"Yes, dear," Sandy said, half sarcastically and half lovingly, which was his way of saying he would make it happen.

They both relaxed and kissed with a short hug.

"And don't wake the kids when you're leaving. I want to enjoy my coffee and think about my garden."

"Yes, dear," Sandy added for insurance.

Allison saw his car pull away through the living room window from where she sat at the kitchen table. The house was quiet save for the ticking of the kitchen clock. She looked down at her garden magazine and gently touched the cover that featured a backyard picture of spring daffodils and tulips, imaging a similar arrangement for her own backyard. She smiled, thinking Sandy had bought her the magazine the last time he went to the grocery store, but wondered if he really understood all what was involved in maintaining a garden, or what was involved in work around the home for that matter. In times past, they argued about the equal distribution of chores, with Sandy feeling his major contribution to building a rec room in the basement for the kids to play or even weekly lawn mowing matched Allison's daily commitment to laundry, cooking and cleaning. But there was more that still bothered Allison. It was the fact that Sandy didn't acknowledge the time and energy demanded in caring for the kids, especially given the irony of his own police work with children and families. She felt alone often.

Nicole recently asked her, "Mommy, how come you are so quiet? Don't you like living here?"

Allison was shocked.

"Of course I do, honey. I love being here with our family. There is no other place in the whole world I would rather be. Why do you ask, sweetheart?"

"Sometimes I see you looking out the window and you look like you want to fly away like a bird."

Allison never told Sandy about this conversation. At the time she had no way to respond to their daughter's question, other than giving Nicole a long, reassuring hug. Nicole skipped away happily but Allison continued to reflect on what her daughter obviously observed in her.

"Like a bird," she thought. Fragile and light, giving voice to a melodious song, graciously and without expectation. Was that how she saw herself? Instead, Allison often felt resentful, giving away her time and energy for Sandy and the kids without remembering what her own voice sounded like. Not like the birds who cheered her while she worked in her garden, but more like a creature always out of reach, wary of flying too close to others for fear of being hurt. Like a bird whose instincts prompted it when the seasons change to migrate somewhere far away. Was that what Nicole saw? A mother who would leave? Did Timmy see the same thing? Did Sandy?

Allison got up and refilled her coffee from the carafe, reaching for the milk in the fridge quietly so as not to make noise and wake the children. They were up way past their bedtimes last night watching a movie on the couch with popcorn as a Friday night treat, hoping to see Daddy before they went to bed. For all Sandy's shift work and late evenings, she never once heard the kids asking if their Dad was ever coming back. They felt secure in his presence, and yet she was with the kids all weekend long and every evening after picking them up at the sitters. Even then, Nicole still wondered if her mother was longing to fly away. Allison marveled at her daughter's perception and at the same time was terrified in feeling so exposed before a four-year-old. No, she was not leaving anywhere, this she knew. But what did she long to give voice to, and to become? It threatened her that a little girl could see that question written on the lines of her mother's face that Allison was barely conscious of herself.

She sat very still in the kitchen for a while, savouring her coffee. She did not want to wake the kids, in part because she could not bear being further exposed this morning. Certainly not by young children who depended on her to be strong, to keep her family together under her wing. "I do long," she admitted to herself. "Nicole is right. I long to be held reassuringly, to make my insecurities fly away and those feelings to never come back."

She glanced down again at her magazine cover, smiling again at the garden image that Sandy always encouraged and believed possible with her gifts. Here, too, she knew she belonged. She felt a renewed sense of warmth as the sun rose above the yard's glistening cedars from last night's rain, radiating through the kitchen window. Her wavy brown hair looked translucent in the sunlight, reflecting the lightness of colour she felt arising within. She got up again and pulled out the frying pan below the stove to prepare breakfast for the kids, whom she expected to get up soon despite the quiet of the house. They would be aroused anyways by the smell of bacon and pancakes which, following the popcorn the evening before, was their favourite weekend meal. It would also facilitate getting everyone outside. If she was lucky, the kids wouldn't be cranky and would want to play in the yard.

Allison was also eager to get to her garden, imaging all kinds of ways of involving Timmy and Nicole in the day's activities, especially since the sun was going to be out. No doubt the sprinkler would provide some effective distraction if it warmed up enough. She imagined the birds singing and keeping them company all day long until Sandy got home.

★ ★ ★

It took Sandy only twenty-five minutes to get downtown, as the west-bound early Saturday morning traffic was fairly light. He called Tanis again en route and asked if she wanted coffee, and arranged to meet at Starbuck's around the corner from the care facility.

"You look like hell," he said as he added half-and-half cream to his coffee. "How was your dad?"

"The same," answered Tanis flatly, as if to say it was anything but the same. She sipped from her coffee, looking away. The coffee shop was busy. Sandy held the door open for a young man who entered as they stepped outside onto the sidewalk.

"So many people coming and going," thought Tanis enviously, "oblivi-ous to what is going on in other's lives."

She wondered if anyone besides Sandy would have noticed how tired she looked this morning. Tired of everything. Then again, if it were not her dad or the cases she worked, what else could she attribute the cause for the overwhelming sense of fatigue she felt? If for any reason, she needed these burdens to avoid looking any further within.

"Care to talk about it?" Sandy asked while they walked to the car. He could not see her face.

"Not really." It came more curtly than Tanis intended. Not wanting it to hang over them, she turned and added quickly, "Well, maybe later. But you can tell me about the case."

Sandy relaxed. It was easier to keep everything on the professional level with Tanis. Even though they had philosophical differences in their approach to police work, he'd rather debate those issues than risk showing a side to his emotional world that seemed to come so easy to him last evening in the quiet and protective darkness of his home, looking tenderly at his young children. He was grateful for how things went this morning with Allison, consciously recommitting in his mind not to be late.

"A woman was found deceased on the Expo Line at the Broadway station last night just after midnight with postpartum hemorrhage. Preliminary reports indicate she died within eight to twelve hours of vaginal birth. There was no baby with her, and no identification, other than her purse with some odd things. Lipstick, keys, a couple condoms, a few plastic containers of cheap hand creams I think, and an embroidered scarf in her coat pocket. It was initialed, umh, let's see," he paused, consulting his notepad, "with the initials a-n-h. No one has reported her missing. A real unknown, like the baby. They're running blood and DNA tests to determine if she's our baby's mother."

Tanis got in the car first while Sandy walked around to the driver's side, waiting for a car to pass on Davie Street. While she was buckling her seatbelt as Sandy got in, he added, "There's one thing, though. The blue coat she was wearing turns out to be pretty common thrift shop apparel."

"That should narrow our search in Vancouver," Tanis quipped.

"You would think, but there was a cash receipt in the right pocket from a place called Stewart's on Hastings near the Army and Navy. The receipt was dated March eighteenth, so not even two weeks ago. The place opens at nine."

"Guess we know where to start."

Tanis was relieved to be in motion. Each block from the care centre gave her emotional distance from what she increasingly experienced of her dad's slow erosion, letting the numbness wash over her again to forget. She didn't want to remember what she saw this morning and each day of late, which only saddened, even repulsed her. To be in motion and focusing on solving a case allowed her to push away the helplessness. Also, to keep at abeyance the other thoughts that came to her mostly in the evenings when she imagined seizing control, to end her dad's suffering. There was no faith in God to comfort her or express vulnerability, which she always envied about Sandy. Nor was there a prayer to take her father to end this indignity. No consoling words to make sense of both his suffering, and her own. In the absence of meaning, what else could she cling to but a wish to have it all over? She relied not on an absent God, but rather her power to deliver her dad of his misery and the misery of her own cycle of desperation and guilt. She willed him dead, but was torn by guilt of harbouring such thoughts while trying to feed him to keep his calorie count up. To be in motion also freed her of the tortured conflict she carried within but could not express out loud, could not lift up in prayer. She resented feeling trapped.

They pulled up in front of the thrift store and entered, approaching a small, ruddy-cheeked man with thin, uneven hair standing behind the cashier's counter. No doubt Stewart himself. He eyed them suspiciously. Sandy spoke first after briefly holding up his police badge.

"Any chance you'd remember selling a Caucasian woman one of your coats fairly recently, shoulder-length straight brown hair, approximately twenty-five years old? She would have appeared pregnant."

"We see lots of people in this place, mister," the vendor answered, "and as long as they pay cash and don't steal anything or cause me trouble, I don't pay much attention to who is who." Stewart breathed noisily through his mouth.

Tanis smiled, thinking to herself that this crusty old man wouldn't care to know anybody if he could help it. It didn't appear like he wanted to engage this conversation much further, nor did she.

"Just how many people buy these cheap blue coats?" Sandy pressed, motioning over to the rack where several of them hung.

"You'd be surprised. Lots of them. Not everybody in town shops at Neiman Marcus."

"But light blue? I see quite an assortment of colours. Dark blue, brown, looks like beige or something. The blue one isn't really the most flattering. Certainly you would notice someone taking one of the blue ones off your hands. God knows not all your stock is swept up by customers."

"Well, maybe I do. What's in it for me?" He perspired under his bulbous nose.

"You get to do your civic duty by helping your fellow man, but of course you are accustomed to doing that already," Sandy shot back. He had little patience for people who either refused to get involved when the only cost was some inconvenience to them, or worse, when it was in exchange for some personal benefit. It sickened him how greasy and transparent people were.

"You think it's fun selling stuff to these people?" the vendor replied. "Every morning there's some bum sleeping in front. I have to kick them and their junk out of the way just so I can open my god damned doors. Or they pretend they're shopping to warm up, trying on stuff with their drug-scarred arms and lice-filled hair, spreading disease all over my store."

"No doubt you must feel pretty good about yourself when you go home at the end of the day after exploiting the poor, you asshole."

"Fuck you!" Stewart replied, looking Sandy in the eye without wavering, his heavy breath punctuating the stand-off.

"Alright you two," Tanis intervened. She looked at Sandy with a 'what the hell are you doing?' look on her face. "If there is anyone who has the right to be mad at the world this morning," she thought, "it's me."

Sandy looked over at the coat rack, gathering his composure.

"Anything? You would have sold it on a Wednesday morning, about two weeks ago."

"There were a couple of people in here looking at coats and buying a bunch of other stuff. He got it for her. She didn't want it but he insisted. Kept telling her it would keep her warm, or some damn thing. She was pretty well street trash and he looked like her pimp or sugar daddy or something. As long as they pay I don't care."

"Yeah, yeah. Have you seen them before?" Sandy continued.

"Not the pimp, they keep a low profile, but she's a regular whore around here. They all are."

"You know where she may live?" Tanis asked, knowing they weren't going to get much further with old man Stewart.

"What do I look like, their welfare officer? Why don't you ask their own people? They start turning tricks as soon as they've had their morning coffee around here."

"You would know," Sandy said. "Thank you very fucking much."

They left the store, Tanis instinctively in the lead to hold the door for fear Sandy would slam it behind him. Half the time she felt he was her biggest client. She was still trying to figure out what could set him off so easily in a rage. She hated having to walk on egg shells around him. She always wondered what his wife saw in him.

"Listen, Sandy." She stopped him on the sidewalk in front of the car, making sure they were out of sight of Stewart's. "If we're going to work well together, you have to keep a lid on some of your own shit."

"You think that prick deserves my respect?"

"That prick may be all we have at the moment. You're not going to change him Sandy, so you might as well work him."

He didn't say anything and just got in the car, making no effort to disguise his anger.

She sighed in exasperation, waiting a moment before getting in herself. She put her seat belt on in silence, searching for the right words so as not to come across with a condescending tone. "I have been working with these kinds of guys for a long time. I try to see a bit of their own weakness behind their facade. He is an asshole, for sure, but is he always? I look for that part of their story that if we hit upon it may actually yield more practical results. I'm not talking about being his best friend, but just looking for that angle."

"Seems like everyone is looking for angles."

"Don't we all? You think you or I don't have hurts that we protect and hide from the world? Some people are angry and miserable, yes, but you have to work with that."

She stopped short. Sandy put the car in gear and pulled into traffic. It was time to leave this conversation and move on. Out of respect for her partner, she didn't want to lecture him. Besides, she felt her own miserable attempts to live what she preached, and knew Sandy could easily probe her with personal questions, which she was not prepared to go at that moment, if ever.

They drove in silence for a few blocks before Tanis suggested, "Let's go see my contact over at the shelter. She knows all the women on the street."

★ ★ ★

"A light blue coat? Like 'I'm still a working girl trying to make a living but don't call me a whore' fashion-statement? Listen honey, there are *lots* of girls who have horizons set far and long but their day to day reality is right here on the Eastside. The coats all blend in with their lifestyle."

"April, we're talking recently. The last two or three weeks. It would have stood out," Tanis emphasized.

She looked at April, trying to discern if she was hiding something herself or just not wanting to get involved. They stood in the entranceway of the Downtown Eastside Women's Shelter where April had come out from behind the security glass partition window upon Sandy and Tanis' arrival. The building smelled of bleach and musty tile. Another clerk sat behind the glass in the small office, talking jovially to a resident on the inside hallway of the shelter, whom Tanis recognized from the street. The resident was probably no more than forty, Tanis figured, but the hardened lines on her gaunt face made her look much older and brittle. Her eyes were vacant, without light, despite her broad smile of missing, decaying teeth she revealed uninhibitedly as she joked with the staff member. It was a look all too familiar on the Eastside. April stood with her hands in her jean's front pockets, rocking from side to side on the inside step of her runners, weighing the question.

There were many stories on the street that were unremarkable, thought April, including her own. She was aware that the clients they housed all donned some tragically flawed blue coat of one kind or another, signifying a common past, like a tattoo they could not completely erase. They belonged to an alumni in which their membership was paid at the hands of another.

April had reached for new horizons herself after having first been a frequent resident of the shelter, then volunteering her services to get a leg up before becoming a paid supervisor. She had been clean for seven years now, but still participated in regular recovery groups and other wellness programs to heal her past. The coat she continued to cast off was the memory of her uncle. She was first molested at age five after coming to live with her aunt and uncle when her parents were killed in a motor vehicle accident. Her dad was drunk and ran their car into a tree on the Williams Lake First Nation Reserve in northern BC near 150 Mile House. April and her two older brothers were sent to different relatives, and she only saw her brothers occasionally after that.

She had only faint memories of life before her parents were killed and the family split up. It was as if her childhood began at age five, only to end shortly after. At first, Aunty Mabel tried to protect her niece from her groping husband, making sure she stayed awake until after her husband passed out from drinking. But whenever Aunty Mabel drank herself, April became scared as her protector succumbed to the inevitable drunken arguments and physical fights with her uncle. Aunty Mabel would withdraw to her own room battered and in tears, not emerging for a couple days, leaving April and her cousins to defend themselves. Her uncle would become enraged by his wife's withdrawal, which he interpreted as punishment, and grabbed whomever he felt. He was completely random, which made his abuse even more terrifying as none of the children knew who he would choose to molest. April learned it was best not to fight back, to keep what was left to herself deep inside, away from others, locked away in a secret room like her Aunty.

Over time, with the recurring cycle of abuse and abandonment, there was little left inside worth hiding. All she felt was a terrible sense of shame and unworthiness. She saw herself as wrong, a mistake of humanity beyond redemption. Even after her uncle died in her mid-teens following a cerebral bleed he sustained when falling backwards off a low level deck while drunk, the pain never let up for April. She was glad he was dead and shed no tears at his funeral. She carried on as if nothing happened. For years she pretended, hiding her pain even after she went to work at 150 Mile House and met a boy who helped her forget, who told her he loved her. When he left her once he had his fill, and another boy in turn told her he loved her before he left too, she buried her pain further. Unlike Aunty Mabel, it took April years to finally emerge from her secret room.

She carried the weight of not feeling good enough, always somehow tragically flawed, until she befriended the sweet peace of smoked crack, washing over her like a warm blanket of love. In that first encounter with her new lover, she finally felt like she belonged. It was a family she could call her own, not realizing until later that it would own her and keep her locked away. She would find momentary reprieve from her pain, struggling to come out of her only room to test if the world could ever be a trustworthy place. After using crack, the shame and hurt would return with a vengeance, like her uncle in his rage, grabbing hold of her soul. The physical withdrawal was as painful as the memory of Aunty Mabel's emotional withdrawal when she was no longer capable to care for her children.

Now in her forties herself, like the vacant eye resident, April bore the ravages of prolonged drug use and the sex trade work that supported her habit. Her eyes had light, but more of a concealed rage than joy. She is among the few whose revolving door experience of treatment and relapse eventually led to a cautious recovery, thanks to skilled medical care, counseling and the unconditional support of others. She has tried to emulate those supporters in her work with the women on the street. The scars of an embittered life remain, as do enduring patterns of mistrust and bitterness. She was not always able to be emotionally present to others and struggled with sustaining long-term relationships with men without old patterns sabotaging her own happiness. She could not return to the streets, but also did not feel ready to leave the Eastside. The thought of completely leaving behind any semblance of her past life, as destructive as it was, terrified her.

Conversations with Tanis always seemed to force her to look beyond her own current horizon.

"There's no one here wearing that coat but I saw a girl who goes by the name of Cherry Blossom who has one. Not much of a spring time blossom, if you ask me," April couldn't resist adding.

"Where does she live?" Sandy asked.

April turned from Tanis to Sandy, then back to Tanis again, addressing her as if he didn't exist. She didn't care much for Sandy.

"Probably around Gore Street. She hangs out close to Chinatown to turn tricks for the Orient fetish market. Works the streets with the others."

"Others?" asked Tanis.

"Asians."

"She's Asian? As in Chinese, Korean or Japanese?" Sandy shot back, taking on an increasingly interrogating tone.

Without looking at him, she replied matter-of-factly, "She's Vietnamese. Her family came over with the other boat people, I'm told, but she's Canadian. You can tell. I also heard she had a brother with ties to one of the local youth gangs who was killed. But I'm not sure if that's just bullshit. Just stuff I heard from one of my sources who wasn't all that reliable. But I've long lost those connections now anyways," she said, turning to eye Sandy, "and I wouldn't care to know them."

Tanis looked at Sandy briefly to acknowledge that piece of information. They both knew she obviously wasn't the woman, and probably not the baby's mother, either.

Tanis continued. "Anyone you know around here who would have been pregnant?"

April's eyes widened. "You're talking about the woman found on the SkyTrain last night, aren't you? The radio said she was the one who left her baby in a church."

Sandy spoke up. "Yeah, we're trying to identify the woman on the train. What we can say is she was found wearing a blue coat linked to a store in this neighbourhood. She was Caucasian, with dark hair and few possessions, which is pretty much all we have. Any ties involving the other case you heard about are merely speculative media reports."

April looked directly at Sandy. "Right," she said flatly. She added encouragingly, "Well, it can't be her anyways, as I saw Cherry Blossom this morning."

"Where?" Sandy asked.

"Same place you were this morning on your way to work." She motioned to Tanis' Starbucks cup that she still carried, unfinished, with a lipstick stained rim. "Saw her from the window when I was getting my own coffee. She was heading up East Pender on the way to Chinatown. And she wasn't wearing no blue coat. This one was brown with a cheap fur collar. A step up, but not by much."

Residents at the shelter often complained that April was judgmental, and felt she looked down on others with disdain. April always made Sandy uncomfortable as if he was looking at himself in a mirror.

"Chinatown," Sandy repeated. He started to leave, to get away from April's accusatory eyes.

"Thanks, April," added Tanis. If you hear anything about a missing person or someone having a baby, or even rumours of someone trying to hide her pregnancy, let us know, okay?"

"Will do." While she had little patience for those abusing or manipulating others in their pursuit of drugs, for which she was a self-described master manipulator herself, she was not unsympathetic to the needs of pregnant women. She had several miscarriages herself, viewing the losses and subsequent sterility as a result of recurrent chlamydia infections as another painful reminder of her past, and a lost opportunity for the family she could not have.

Sandy and Tanis drove the eight blocks to the strip near Chinatown that April mentioned. It was not hard to find her. Neither Tanis nor Sandy were fazed seeing sex trade workers on the streets at ten-thirty in the morning, and there standing among them was Cherry Blossom with her cheap fur collar, bantering with people in cars slowing down to take a look. They pulled alongside the woman as Tanis spoke from the window of the car in a casual, non-threatening tone so she wouldn't run.

"Got time for coffee, Cherry Blossom?" She displayed her badge, adding quickly, "We'll buy you lunch."

"Hey man, what about us?" called another worker, and others cajoled and teased Cherry Blossom when she guardedly approached the car.

"What do you want, cops?"

"We just want to ask you a few questions," Tanis said.

"Can't you see I'm busy?"

"Can't see you girls having much business while we're here anyways." Few johns would mistake an unmarked police car with a couple people in the front seat. "Won't take us long to talk. Apparently there's a coffee shop not far from here."

Cherry Blossom peered in to look at Sandy. He looked handsome and decent enough, she thought, arousing her curiosity. Besides, she was hungry.

"Sure, business is always slow the morning after a Canucks game. It's the night before and right after that we're busy."

"You get to any games?" Sandy asked as Cherry Blossom got in the back seat.

"Nah, it's not my thing." She opened her purse and took out a compact and lipstick. "I just pretend I'm interested when guys start talking players or playoff chances or stuff like that."

"That sounds pretty knowledgeable," Sandy replied while looking in his rear view mirror at a red light. She applied her lipstick, not looking up.

"Some guy I know is always talking sports. I just work him real hard so he comes and then I take what's owing me and get the hell out."

"You must hate overtime then," Sandy laughed, a little too loud. Evidently, he was pleased with his own joke.

"Like last night."

"Wow, I am impressed. I wish my wife knew as much about hockey." Tanis turned to look back at Cherry Blossom in the rear seat, rolling her eyes. Cherry Blossom smiled. Tanis thought there was some level of connection women shared, regardless of the circumstances.

"Well, a good looking guy like you, I'm sure we can arrange something. I have been known to go three ways."

"I'm afraid the only three ways I do is keeping up with my wife and two kids."

"You just keep my name in case you change your mind. What did you say your names were again?"

"I'm sorry," Tanis apologized. Her face blushed as if she violated the woman's Charter rights.

Sandy quickly introduced himself and his partner with the same levity in his voice. Tanis was amazed at how intuitive he was, knowing how to keep people engaged and to help build trust when he wanted. She stopped short of thinking he would have made a good social worker though, especially after the disastrous clinic he ran at Stewart's.

"That's real polite of you, but I think you wanted to ask me more than simply about the Canucks' game last night," chirped Cherry Blossom. They pulled up in front of the coffee shop.

"Got to hand it to you, guys," she added nervously when no one answered, "you get all the good parking spots." She got out of the car with Tanis and waited until Sandy walked around from the side to join them on the sidewalk.

"What do you really want?" She was serious now. Cherry Blossom didn't take any further steps. The tone of conversation changed immediately.

Tanis spoke, turning to face her. Sandy glanced up and down the sidewalk. The look on his face changed, too.

"Do you own a blue coat that you would have recently bought from Stewart's?"

"Suppose I do? What's a coat got to do with anything?"

"We're investigating a case in which it would help to know the owner of the coat."

"I don't remember. I own lots of coats. Do you like this one?" Her voice faltered.

Sandy drew a breath and motioned to speak, but Tanis interrupted, trusting her own instincts.

"What's your name? Before this I mean, and the street?"

The woman hesitated, looking at Tanis before responding, sizing her up. She learned you had to be careful getting into a car on the street, but even more so with engaging certain conversations. Tanis waited patiently for her response, managing to hold eye contact with her. Cars rushed past.

"Actually, it is Cherry Blossom. In Vietnam, my real name is Mai Ly, which translated means cherry blossom. But no one calls me that. My English name fits better with all this," motioning to the people on the sidewalk.

"What about friends? I'm sure you have some friends, people you can trust," Tanis pressed.

Mai Ly stiffened.

"I have friends," she replied defensively.

"Friends who confide in you?"

"Lots of girls tell me things in private. I don't go snooping but I guess they look up to me. I have been around. I know things."

"What about friends who are in trouble? Do people come and tell you things if they were in trouble?"

"I don't get what you're asking. What do you really want?"

Tanis paused, looking at her partner quickly. Sandy sensed it too. She didn't know what happened.

"Mai Ly, did you lend or give your blue coat to anyone, someone who confided in you?" Tanis' voice was soft. She added, "It's okay, you didn't do anything wrong. You can tell us."

Mai Ly pulled nervously at her hair, looking down the street, as if she was going to take off.

Sandy started again to speak, and again Tanis interrupted.

"Mai Ly, it's okay. We just want to know who you gave the coat to. We are trying to identify someone."

"Identify someone! What do you mean? Is she okay?"

"You gave your coat to another girl? What's she look like?"

"She's tall, kinda skinny. She has straight dark hair like me but thicker, with more body. She's really pretty"

"Pretty like you? Like a cherry blossom too?" Sandy interjected.

Mai Ly eyed him and reddened with anger.

"No!" Mai Ly shot back. "Not like me, she's... she's good."

"You mean she's not in the sex trade?" Tanis continued.

"Not really. I mean, she's here. She's new. We're trying to look out for her."

"What's her name?"

"Magda."

"Does she have a last name?"

"I don't know. I never asked. I told you I don't go snooping. They tell me what they want and I don't ask any more."

"Did she say if she had family, other friends who look out for her?"

"Like I said, she's new. Been here since the fall. Right when it got cold and rainy. But I don't really know much about her, other than she's running. We're all running from something."

"What about you, Mai Ly? What are you running from?" Sandy asked.

"The only thing you need to know is I should be running back to work," she said offhandedly. "I thought you were going to get me lunch?"

Tanis looked her straight in the eye and put her hand on her arm. Mai Ly pulled away.

"Mai Ly. We found a woman on the SkyTrain last night. She was bleeding a lot. When people noticed her, she was already gone. We think she was wearing your blue coat. We think it could be Magda."

Mai Ly gasped, bringing both her hands to her mouth. She looked bewildered. The tough street-wise woman suddenly looked helpless, not in control. Sandy and Tanis stood next to her, still feet from the parked car on the sidewalk. People continued to come and go from the coffee shop behind them.

"There's more, Mai Ly. We think she may have had a baby. She may have died shortly after childbirth, giving birth on her own. Did you know she was pregnant?"

"Pregnant?" No way. She didn't look pregnant to me."

"Did she ever talk about someone? Someone she may have been with? Maybe the baby's father?" Tanis led with all the questions now.

"No, nothing. I don't know anything. Can we eat now? I got to get back to work."

"Sure, Mai Ly, let's get something to eat," Tanis said. "But after lunch we may need you to help ID her, if no other family can be found. Will you do that for us?"

"It won't take long," said Sandy. "We would just need to drive over to St. Paul's Hospital. We'll get you back to work in an hour."

Tanis was hungry and knew she was in no position to negotiate.

"Well, since you are costing me money, how about throwing in money for supper, too?"

"Absolutely," assured Tanis. "I have to go make a few phone calls to the hospital first and you and Officer Kohler can go start getting some food."

"Before we do that, I just want to ask you another question," said Sandy authoritatively. He had enough being in the backseat. He wanted them to both know it was his case.

"We found a cloth on her, I mean, in your coat pocket. A fancy white lace scarf. With initials *a-n-h* on it. Do you know if that means anything? Perhaps some keepsake from family, a last name, anything?"

"It's not her scarf. It's mine. I lent it to her. She was crying."

"Out of curiosity, what do the initials stand for?" Sandy asked.

"I have no idea. I got it from a priest."

CHAPTER 9

Stephen Nichols was feeling pretty good about himself at lunch. On the contrary, Marie tried to identify why she did not share the confidence exuding from his large, expansive frame. As the social justice committee members stood in line for the catered food brought in for the retreat, she mulled over the sometimes heated exchange between members that had transpired earlier that morning, wondering just when it was that she began to detach from the conversation. Others were quiet too, making Stephen's animated presence even more overbearing. He laughed heartily, unaware of or at least indifferent to its impact on others near him, including his wife, who intentionally drifted further back in line.

Marie looked up vacantly at the high basement ceiling windows in the parish hall where the social justice retreat was held, as if to reach up and pull down what little natural light was able to filter in. Hoping to draw the rays close to fill the emptiness in the room, and in her life. The bright fluorescent lights in the basement hall reflected starkly off the linoleum floor, washing out the soft, vibrant colours of the liturgical banners hung along the walls, much as Marie felt her own light being eclipsed by Stephen. The rows of ceiling lights now hummed noticeably like a mocking, electric laugh above the muted conversations in line, magnifying the volume of the different voices in Marie's head, neither of them her own.

Besides Stephen and those who privately shared his sense of victory, it was a very different atmosphere now compared to the beginning of the retreat when the collective nervous energy of the group betrayed at least some optimism of finding common ground. Marie was grateful for the opportunity to talk with Fr. Bao as the committee members arrived for coffee before the retreat started.

"Did you manage to get much sleep last night with all the commotion, Fr. Bao?"

"I would be lying to you if I said I got a full night's sleep. I don't think the police left before eleven. And I still had to do a little more preparation for today, so it was late when I went to bed." Fr. Bao was cheerful but could not hide his fatigue owing from another restless night.

"Thank you for organizing this day," Marie offered. "I know it takes a lot of work."

He smiled, but said nothing.

She added cautiously, "I'm glad we didn't cancel. It's important. We need to talk about options and find what's right for this parish."

"I agree. But I think we're still far apart on some issues, I'm afraid." He stopped short, pausing to sip from his coffee.

He was about to continue when Marie asked, "Fr. Bao, do you mind me asking when you first got the idea for a community kitchen? I don't think I recall you ever saying, or at least I don't remember."

Fr. Bao studied Marie's face, wondering in turn if he ever recalled talking to her alone before. He saw she was genuinely curious, which surprised him. Marie was surprised by her own question too.

"You're right, I'm not sure if I ever did say. My adoptive parents helped organize a similar project in their parish in Manitoba a number of years ago, although on a much smaller scale. They lived in a small rural town but there were still some people falling through the cracks. You know how hard rural life can be, especially when the economy crashes. I got the idea from their parish."

Marie wanted to ask more about their model, how it was funded, and the kinds of client needs they served. Instead she asked, "Do you see them very often?"

Fr. Bao looked directly at her, taken back. He looked pained. There were many responses he thought of afterwards that could have easily satisfied Marie's curiosity but lamely said instead, "Oh, of course, in fact they're coming to spend Easter with me at the parish. I will introduce them to you if we get the chance."

"That would be really good, Fr. Bao. I'd love to meet them." Marie didn't know what else to say. She smiled awkwardly before taking her seat. Fr. Bao was relieved when another committee member came up to him to say hello. Marie continued to watch Fr. Bao reflectively while Stephen bantered with other members before joining her at the table once the retreat was called to order. She wondered about Fr. Bao's family, and her own.

The retreat began with prayer and the usual housekeeping details. Marie avoided eye contact with the others. Without looking, she knew Stephen was becoming quieter and intense, no doubt fixated on every word Fr. Bao said, looking for any sign of weakness to exploit. She had met those critical eyes before, and knew what would follow. She blamed herself, feeling responsible for what happened, and angry at herself for not challenging Stephen without backing down. She did not have to look at him to know what was coming over his face. Nor did she did not want to look at him when he was readying for a fight, to be reminded of her own vulnerability in the face of the other council members he would soon be confronting. It was as much dread as it was resentment that turned her gaze away.

The agenda focused primarily on the outreach proposals, beginning with the community soup kitchen as part of the five-point parish plan. Fr. Bao briefly reviewed the purpose, business case details, and timelines before calling for discussion. He spoke dispassionately but firmly in his role as chair, lending confidence to the proposal. Predictably, Stephen was the first to respond, adding his own persuasive critique. He argued the parish outreach soup kitchen would be difficult to manage given the labour costs if they were going to run it seven days a week as proposed. He acknowledged the parish was fairly stable despite declining envelope collections. And while the mortgage was paid off, he added, and the roof project was nearly complete, it was the competing parish commitments that were going to be the issue.

"I discussed the impact of the proposal with the Archbishop in my conversation with him last week, and shared my concern that other existing priorities in the parish would suffer if they were spread too thin," he explained.

"For example?" asked Fr. Bao.

"For example, the Archbishop's pastoral vision to engage the youth in the diocese and his support of more comprehensive educational programs."

"What about our commitments to the poor, and our mandate as a social justice subcommittee of the parish council?" Fr. Bao asked calmly, wanting to explore Stephen's and the rest of the committee's understanding of their role and how best it be achieved. He genuinely wanted to hear about everyone's vision.

Stephen was prepared. While he did not stand, he filled his place at the table opposite Fr. Bao, sitting square to him with his arms folded across his chest. Not in a menacing or defiant manner, but with the casual confidence of a man who felt grounded in his truth. He drew in a loud, deep breath before responding.

"We also have a commitment to be responsible. To be good stewards. It's a more effective use of resources to consolidate our efforts around the existing Archdiocesan downtown initiatives, channeling our limited parish capital and time to leverage what is already in place versus starting something brand new. Besides, a community soup kitchen requires a separate hospitality and food handling permit, infection control practices, let alone ongoing training and supervision of an already scarce supply of volunteers."

He felt the momentum changing, adding, "Need I point out to committee members that such a project would increase demand for food storage capacity when we are already committed to a building plan footprint to renovate and expand the classroom space, as well as increase parking to accommodate the growing number of families in the parish?"

Stephen did not let up.

"And do we even have a current needs assessment? I suggest we review additional city and Archdiocesan studies on the need for community kitchens before committing further parish resources. For all we know, existing social programs may already have that covered."

"We know from our own parish records there is a wide disparity of wealth among the families, and it is definitely growing," maintained Fr. Bao. "Along with the growth in disparity among the parish families St. Benedict's serves in general, there are more parishioners living in subsidized housing projects within a few kilometers radius. And that's just parishioners. Of course, there are even more people at risk throughout Collingwood."

He paused briefly to sip from the coffee cup he had been cradling in his hands. As skilled a debater Stephen was, Fr. Bao knew how to take advantage of pauses in a conversation for strategic effect.

Before Stephen could respond, Fr. Bao emphasized, "Yes, I admit, there are a few wealthy neighbourhoods along the Renfrew Ravine Park in Collingwood for example, where other professionals like you and Marie live, Stephen, but overall you can't ignore that the community around the parish has become economically challenged. Look at our committee decision a couple years ago to sponsor the clothing bin on the parish property along the Euclid Avenue hall entrance. And to think how radical that seemed at the time. I was even skeptical to commit parish resources to operate it. But how many bags are left in or around it every week, destined to be sold for discount prices at the thrift shops on Kingsway?"

Stephen was not dissuaded. "The socioeconomic disparity of the Eastside demands more of our entire church's resources than we could ever realize on our own. But if we could pool our efforts, it will have a greater proportionate impact. Besides, investing in the youth of the parish to ensure they have a good moral foundation is what will best prevent the very hardships we all want to avoid. We have to think in terms of the long haul."

"Do you really believe that, Stephen?" asked Ann Lee, another founding parishioner who held a Simon Fraser University faculty appointment in applied sciences. "If I didn't know any better, I would think that you just don't want the poor in our own backyard."

"I won't deny my opinion that community soup kitchens can breed a system of entitlement unless accompanied by a comprehensive set of social programs, which the parish is in no position to provide, assuming we could even operate a viable community kitchen."

Ann looked incredulously at Stephen.

"That is exactly what the soup kitchen intends to do, representing the first of many parish strategies to provide a range of comprehensive services for their neighbourhood. I have reviewed the urban studies research that Paul Wheaton has done at Simon Fraser and it works. It's about starting somewhere and creating a movement for others to build and improve upon."

"That's really all we're talking about," echoed Fr. Bao. "I think the research Ann has reviewed is encouraging. I see St. Benedict's serving as a catalyst of transformation in the community. It has to start somewhere and I'd just as well like to see it be our parish taking leadership. I'm totally fine if we haven't figured out all the details and take a chance on serving the poor. Each day we wait is another day a potential family goes without. I can't accept that."

"Neither can I," said Ann. She sat up straight as though to punctuate her position. She was about to go on when Stephen interrupted.

"Jumping in too soon can threaten the viability of the parish if it sucks dry all our resources. Out of respect for the poor, I think we owe it to them to be able to follow through on something we started versus getting people's hopes up and dashing their expectations, which is cruel. Instead, let's put our efforts in our own kids where we know we can make a sustained impact."

Marie turned abruptly in her chair.

Stephen glared at her, then turned back to Fr. Bao to add, "That was the mindset original parishioners like Marie and me took when we first built St. Benedict's long before you arrived. And now look at where we are. We can't risk jeopardizing our continued presence in the community, or overlook our children."

Fr. Bao replied, "I say we can't risk jeopardizing our service to the poor, which is the reason for having a parish in the first place, in my mind."

"Is it, Father?" Stephen challenged.

Marie looked at her husband, clearly annoyed. It was Ann who answered.

"I might not be able to explain it as well as Fr. Bao, even though I too am an original parishioner," she couldn't resist emphasizing, "but what I see is an opportunity to make a difference in the community. To reach out to even one person and actually do the kind of things we hear about in the Gospels. Jesus didn't have a sustainability strategy," she added sarcastically, "He just went out and touched the poor."

"Ann, we can't be naive. There is nothing inherently wrong with living the Gospel *and* having a good business plan. As a lawyer involved with other successful community projects, I couldn't counsel otherwise. Again, what I worry about is raising expectations and then causing more harm than good."

"I agree," said Fr. Bao with a conciliatory tone. "No one wants that. And yet, we all want to be a parish that is faithful to what we preach, even if we make mistakes along the way. You ask if that means taking a chance on serving the poor, and I say yes, absolutely."

"Mistakes," said Stephen flatly.

"Yes, mistakes. But at least it's about doing something. And we can still provide for good catechetical programs. We can do both. We can teach our kids a lot about making a difference in serving the poor by getting them involved with our outreach ministry. To model what it means to be a community. What better way to illustrate the Gospel in action?"

Fr. Bao continued. "There is a certain wisdom about grass root initiatives. Ann and I have gone to a lot of meetings across the city with mental health and other social service professionals to obtain support for the community kitchen proposal. In time, through this network it could help spur community shelters as part of an overall housing first strategy."

"You know, I hear a lot about those housing first concepts," interjected Iain Hutchinson, who had been among the committee members watching the debate unfold. Iain was visibly impatient, mustering his courage despite his faltering voice.

"But I am no less clear what it really means here. It is at best a good idea, maybe even a virtuous one. What I am really clear about, however, is that Stephen has recommended consolidating our efforts into supporting something that we know one hundred per cent is working and where a legitimate need exists."

He looked around the table and saw people were listening, giving him more confidence.

"Also, where we already have identified parish volunteers and stand the best chance for success with educational programs, versus initiating a project based on a yet to be validated business plan when there is no guarantee we can be successful. We need more than people with big hearts. We can still contribute to the existing downtown projects, but as far as our own parish pastoral plan, I second Stephen's motion that we instead undertake a capital project to add space to the classrooms, which are already sadly under capacity. That will allow us to build for the future."

"The future you speak of is for the privileged, Iain. What about those who don't even have the everyday basics?" replied Ann. Iain looked down. His brief moment of courage faded.

"The children of our parish have a need for catechesis," Stephen answered, as much for himself as for Iain.

"And other children in our community have a need for food in their stomach. Which do think is the living the Gospel?" Ann shot back.

Marie remained silent, nodding occasionally, but was obviously uncomfortable with the escalating conflict, especially when the arguments became more personal. A close friend of the Nichols, Linda Thomas, a Jamaican-born business woman in the community, joined in the debate, asking Fr. Bao if they were spending too much time pursuing social justice efforts for the poor when their own parishioners did not have timely access to the sacraments.

"For example," she added, "last month when you and Fr. Spivak were away at a social justice meeting in Kelowna and unable to preside over Helen James' funeral, we had to bring in another priest in the Archdiocese to cover. And this was a long term member of this parish who helped with many of the same grass root initiatives you described earlier when our parish was young and lots of families needed help. I understood the family had to wait until later in the week when the other parish priest was free, inconveniencing them. Some even flew in from Jamaica and were already pressured to get back to work," Linda challenged. "It was embarrassing."

"How Fr. Spivak and I allocate our time is not up for discussion. We are discussing whether to develop a community soup kitchen offering hot food to the local poor, or as Stephen has alternatively motioned, to instead organize members to volunteer outside the parish in the Downtown Eastside and put our local efforts into building up our classrooms and our youth educational programs."

"How can you compare our neighbourhood with the Eastside, or even what I see in my home country?" said Linda. "We're not anything like East Hastings. Yeah, I agree with Stephen. We are wasting energy trying to create some token program to say we support the poor when there is so much we can do to augment the needed resources to support outreach ministries in downtown Vancouver. Contribute some volunteer hours downtown, yes, but focus our time and money on the needs of our youth right here."

"I wouldn't liken our proposal to mere tokenism," challenged Ann. "Those people we served before did not see our efforts as an empty gesture. How did so many people attend the drop-in last year with donated sandwiches? How did the word get out?"

"Precisely," said Stephen, looking not at Ann for her reaction but that of their parish priest. He continued, "There were people from downtown coming here, when there are already resources for their poor in their own neighbourhood."

Iain jumped in, finding his voice again. "I heard one of the women say you were going to businesses and talking to people on the street in the Eastside, handing out flyers and SkyTrain tickets for people to come here. Is that true, Fr. Bao? Because I'm trying to understand the rationale of promoting a ministry when people don't even live around here. Why would anyone come?"

"I don't know, but explain how a woman managed to make her way here last night," Ann replied, looking at Fr. Bao.

"The same woman who evidently died trying to get back," added Stephen derisively.

"Your point?"

Fr. Bao stayed calm, though he was tempted to weigh in.

"Our point is that there are already other parish needs right in our own community," countered Stephen. "We don't need to be bringing people here. What's the value of that?"

"But that's what we're saying, Stephen," pressed Ann. "Look around you. Go for a walk around the church. Don't just get in your car and drive home after Mass. There is good work we can do right here. There are people looking for a way out of the downtown scene. We can be a transition point, a way forward to help integrate those on the margins into a welcoming and supportive community."

"Look at what happened last night. Where was the good in that? A woman comes to leave her kid here only to die on the SkyTrain on the way home. How is that a step forward? Where's the justice in that?"

The tension in the room was magnified. Ann and Stephen glared at each other. No one spoke. The woman's death seemed to have the final say.

Recollecting himself, Stephen went on, calmly offering his assessment of the events last night. He spoke in a measured and consoling tone.

"I am left to wonder if we may actually be doing more harm in raising expectations among the poor and vulnerable if they assume they can come here for food and hospitality, or even to leave a baby, while the proper and comprehensive care they require goes unaddressed. Look what happened to that woman. You can ask yourself if whether we somehow contributed to her death."

Stephen let his words hang in the air, pausing momentarily, before adding softly,

"Listen, I'm not saying she didn't receive spiritual support, and if Fr. Bao did actually talk to her as the media suggests, no doubt he would have provided her comfort and peace. But the fact of the matter is after she left here she died on the SkyTrain, alone, leaving an infant behind. If she came here from the Eastside thinking the parish would offer her a transition out of the inner city, then all we did was set her up for failure."

"Oh, we failed all right," replied Ann quickly. "We failed her by the very attitudes you so eloquently demonstrate, Stephen. A smug complacency that 'the poor will be with us always.' As long as we say Mass seven days a week, hold catechism classes for the kids and preside over funerals, weddings and baptisms without delay, we have it covered. We don't need to think of improving the lot of others in our own neighbourhood as long as we keep it contained in someone else's."

"Alright now. Let's move on," Fr. Bao finally said.

"Father, just a reminder, there is a motion on the floor, seconded by Iain, that we allocate our parish resources to strengthen existing parish programs and to forgo the community soup kitchen," said Peter Roy. As Treasurer, Peter had reviewed the projected deficit with the downward trend in parish envelope collections that they have been monitoring the past few years, given the broader socioeconomic shifts in the parish community. While there were admittedly more families in the parish, there was less revenue coming in. Peter was open to the community kitchen concept but given his own forecasting of yearly expenses over revenues, he leaned in favour of the motion as the only responsible option.

Fr. Bao asked Peter for clarification of the financial projections. Peter restated his position, adding he would reconsider if there was a more viable business case for annual costs to operate the community kitchen, including the necessary infusion of startup cash to furnish equipment and supplies for the kitchen, as well as promotional advertisement. He pointed out that the proposal did not detail a functional plan for additional services, given the incremental vision for the kitchen as part of a long term outreach strategy to the neighbourhood as Ann and Fr. Bao envisioned.

"Well, what if we pursue potential donors to launch the project, since we will certainly need to do so anyways if we undertake a capital campaign for adding classroom space?" asked Ann. "Either way, we will need to attract dollars. The fact that this is not in place yet shouldn't be a reason to shelve the community kitchen. If we follow that logic, we should be shelving the classroom expansion project until such time we have that money too."

"The difference is that there is less broad base support for a community kitchen. People are afraid," Stephen pointed out. He sat up straight and cleared his throat. Marie looked away.

"Who's afraid, Stephen? Not everyone is scared like you. It's nothing really new. It's about the social gospel, bringing Christ's ministry of healing and compassion in reaching out to the most downtrodden, who, whether you are prepared to admit it or not, do live both downtown as well as in our neighbourhood," Ann declared. "If we partner with other local social service agencies here in Collingwood, we can help share costs. The community kitchen provides a place for people to gather, get a hot meal, and build community. Maybe only then, when people have firsthand experience of hospitality and unconditional acceptance, there may be some means of addressing the accompanying issues of addiction and abuse. That's when referrals for treatment may be possible and other counseling resources. This is the kind of creative thinking that would be really powerful to educate our kids."

She hesitated. At risk of sabotaging her own appeal, she suggested further, "We might even be able to provide a clean needle exchange for IV drug users who are continuing to use."

Ann could not help herself. Her suggestion was already enough to push the envelope, and didn't dare suggest arguments in favour of dispensing condoms as another means to stop the spread of disease, which she knew would shock some parishioners' sensibilities.

Fr. Bao had raised the issue before. He and Ann had researched and heard presentations on some of the innovative programming in the Downtown Eastside, wondering if it would be worth pursuing in their parish. They both knew it was contentious enough and would only enflame the conversation. Fr. Bao felt it would be more strategic to start first with a community kitchen and then address those issues later. However, some of his contacts warned that the reality of the people they planned to serve would make it an issue sooner than later and thus it would be prudent to start discussing it in advance. The first day a client used the washroom after a hot meal and left a dirty needle in the garbage or sink would signal the time had already arrived.

"With all due respect, Father, Marie and I have been reviewing the literature on so-called harm reduction strategies and they are controversial from a scientific perspective, let alone a moral one. There is evidence they actually encourage use."

"Bullshit!" Ann went red in the face, surprised by her own visceral reaction, but looked steadily and menacingly at Stephen nonetheless. She was not going to back down.

"Ann, can I ask that you please watch your language," Fr. Bao intervened, not to curtail the conversation, but to steer it towards a constructive outcome.

"It's alright, Father," said Stephen. "I have read about those counter arguments but the fact is, once you go down that road of aiding a person in their addiction, you are just inviting more use, compounding the very problem you are trying to stop. It's one thing to feed the poor, but the poor don't need us feeding them the means to pursue their habits."

Fr. Bao felt heavy with sadness, looking for the words to salvage what was left of the original proposal. The motion on the floor to veto the kitchen loomed larger. Even normally measured Peter Roy looked uneasy. Marie clenched her hands, looking equally sad and pained by what was just said.

Stephen did not let up. "And then we are going to see more people coming to the neighbourhood to traffic their goods, filling those clean needles with more drugs. What's to say all those dirty needles will go in disposable buckets even if we did put them in the parish washrooms? The more we attract this behaviour, the more we can expect some of those needles to end up in the parks used by the neighourhood kids, including the children of our parish."

Ann attempted to provide her interpretation of the literature that harm reduction strategies actually decrease littering of dirty needles and reduce incidents of transmitting HIV and hepatitis. She talked about some parishes in New Jersey involved with clean needle exchanges that had gathered local support, but it was not broadly supported by the entire Catholic and other faith communities.

"Great, and maybe we should be handing out condoms," Stephen pressed, finishing Ann's thoughts that she herself stopped short voicing a moment ago.

He looked around the room from one to another before resting his gaze on Fr. Bao.

"I am sure, Father, the Church has something important to say about this. Helping the poor is one thing, even addicts, but encouraging fornication and promiscuity is another. We have to look to the future of our parish, educating our youth in Christian values, not promoting even more sinful behaviour. You just have to look at what happens when mothers start to abandon their own babies. It's bad enough in the Eastside, but all we would be doing is spreading the problem."

Fr. Bao saw it was no use debating the issue further. Even Ann seemed to lose her nerve and so to spare prolonged humiliation, Fr. Bao called for a vote to put the matter to rest. He described himself often as an incrementalist, and had already begun to concede defeat to pick up the battle later when he could rally more parish support for the community kitchen. An incrementalist who, only slowly and over many years, felt was able to let go of his family. Yes, it was easier to describe one as such, he admitted, but another thing to live and go on from this place of uncertainty.

The proposal was defeated six to four, but there was an acknowledgement by the social justice committee that they would revisit the proposal if there were substantiated evidence of need and the available financial and human resources to support it. For Fr. Bao, that was all he needed to hear to keep fighting. He remembered his mother's final words to him.

The morning meeting continued for another half hour until noon but it was obvious it had taken the sail out of the retreat, even among those who voted in favour of the motion. Fr. Bao was already a reserved meeting chair, growing more quiet and perfunctory to move through the remaining morning agenda items, not wanting to pursue any unnecessary conversation. After lunch, some of the energy of the group returned as the committee discussed preparations for the upcoming Lenten retreat and the social justice parish reflections. Throughout the afternoon, Stephen attempted to interject some good-natured humour, trying to smooth over tensions, but the group remained divided, largely deferring to Fr. Bao to facilitate discussions.

As the retreat ended, the committee members made their way up the basement hall stairs. The afternoon sun now peered through the parish lobby windows, casting a long shadow. It fell briefly across those who left through the front doors to run Saturday afternoon errands. For others who stayed behind in the lobby, the light invited continued conversation. Fr. Bao joined Linda and Marie as they spoke. Linda held her car keys in hand as if to leave, but turned to Fr. Bao to ask him what she had just been inquiring of Marie to answer.

"Father, do you know anything further of the woman? It must have been pretty upsetting for you."

"Yes, it was. More than you can imagine."

"Maybe not," Marie answered, looking over at Stephen. Stephen was still engaged in a lively discussion with Iain and Peter at the foot of the stairs.

"Well, maybe you will find out more," Linda said as she looked out the side front door windows. "Looks like the police are here again. I think the same ones that were here last night."

They all turned towards the parking lot to see Tanis and Sandy getting out of their car and walking towards the parish entrance door.

CHAPTER 10

Mai Ly looked at Magda's body without saying a word. A brief nod of her head to confirm the dead woman's identity and Mai Ly's civic duty was accomplished. For a moment, Magda was known and remembered. Her voice, her desperation, her secrets, disclosed in confidence with the other women in the early morning hours of a dungy apartment they shared, before sleep or drugs numbed their pain, making them all forget. She did not belong on this metal gurney in the pathology lab any more than she belonged on the streets of the Eastside. The same environment where you were dissected one tendon, one ligament, one memory at a time, barely holding together the broken pieces of your life. Cold and lifeless, exposed for all to see.

Tanis stood next to Mai Ly while the attendant held the sheet respect-fully, pulled back to reveal Magda's head and angular shoulders. Even in death, she looked sad but surprisingly beautiful. Tanis has been in this room many times before, but seldom saw beauty, neither in the morgue nor in her present life. She felt like she was the one lying on the cold metal gurney but lacked the courage to slam the drawer shut behind her, closing a door on her own sadness. She envied her father, who had already started to close a door, shutting her out as her mother had before. Memories of a cherished family also dissected one story at a time.

At least Magda died quickly, not the slow dissipation of joy and meaning that tragic cases and morgue viewings like this had taken from Tanis and what dementia had stolen from her dad. She could not even remember the last time she and her dad shared a laugh. Tanis never could tell him about this part of her job.

At another city hospital, Magda's baby was being held by a volunteer in the neonatal unit, cradling her in a rocking chair. The nursing staff were especially devoted to Baby Jane Doe, barely known like her mother. Unlike Magda's experience, except for what Babcia provided, the baby was already loved and protected. The staff held out hope for their communal baby. Twice in the newborn's two short days of life, she was left with strangers who would not fail her. Magda abandoned her baby a second time by dying, leaving her orphaned. And now, as Mai Ly looked down at Magda's lifeless form, she thought how we had completely and totally abandoned the baby's mother too.

The attendant re-covered her face with the sheet, motioning it is was time to leave.

CHAPTER 11

Stephen knew that his wife was angry. The question was whether to broach the matter in the car on the way home or pretend he didn't notice. During the meeting, she barely glanced at him. Now she looked away completely. They each talked to separate committee members afterwards to avoid standing next to one another. Marie carried on as if Stephen wasn't there, even when he indicated he was ready to go home. They went to their car in silence, Marie walking in front going to the passenger side, waiting for her husband to unlock the door. For a moment, she hesitated before opening her door, wondering if she should get in. The silence was even more pronounced as they drove a few blocks up Joyce Street to Vanness. Stephen reached for the radio and turned on a jazz station, making sure to keep the volume low.

Mustering his nerve, he finally asked, "Something the matter?"

Marie stiffened her lip. "Don't."

"Don't what? Ask you what's the matter?"

"Stephen, let's just forget it."

"Forget about what, Marie? I don't know what you are talking about."

"You know damn well what I'm talking about."

Stephen drove west on Vanness, looking in his side and rear mirror to change lanes, stealing a glance at Marie. He felt his anger rising and stepped down on the accelerator to move into an opening in the right lane.

"What? You mean during the meeting?"

"I said let's drop it."

"No, I want to know."

"You don't want to know. You've already decided what's right. It's fine. Let's just forget about it."

"I wasn't the only one who thought that way. We just want to do what's best for the parish."

"You just want to do what's right for you."

"That's not true. We looked at all sides, you know that. It's what best."

"Is that how you felt about throwing your own son out? To do what's best? For Michael? There, I said it. Is that what you wanted to hear?"

"Oh, don't start with that again!"

"You were the one that wanted to have this conversation, so let's have it. Explain to me how you can talk about children ministries when our own son is walking the streets God knows where."

"Michael is not walking the streets, and you know it. And I was talking about children, not adults who should know better."

"Do I? Do I really know where he lives and how he's managing?"

"He's doing fine. He never fails to let us know when he needs money," Stephen added cynically.

"It's not money he needs. It's his family."

"Oh, he needs money alright. I'm not sure Michael really has much more use for family." Stephen muttered under his breath when stuck behind a slow driver in the right hand lane, then sped around him erratically in time to make the turn north on Earles Street.

"Please slow down," Marie said in a calm but firm voice. Traffic was congested, adding to the tension. She looked out on the sidewalk at a group of young girls, laughing in animated conversation as they walked in front of the storefront windows, shopping bags in tow. She remembered those lazy Saturday afternoons when she was a teen, feeling carefree without ever worrying if there was a place to go home to after, or dreading what waited for her when she did.

"You know, Stephen, I used to think your heart was in the right place, I truly did. But you have to open your eyes and see that not everyone can measure up to your standards. There will be people like Michael, our own son, or even the woman who left her baby who sometimes need help and a little direction, not judgment. Maybe a community kitchen and health clinic is worth pursuing after all."

"So you can redeem yourself? It wasn't just my decision that Michael left. You were a part of it too so don't be putting that on me," he said in a hurtful voice.

"You talk about Michael being the way he is as if it was his choice."

"I know he's different."

"He's gay," Marie added quickly. "Say it, Stephen. He's homosexual and that is the way it is."

"I don't care what he is. That gives him no right to carry on in our house the way he did."

"You had no problem when Rebecca was his age and had parties. You didn't throw her out," Marie shot back.

"Well Becca didn't steal money and lie to us constantly. She grew up and got her education and now look at her. Michael is twenty-three years old and it's high time he grows up."

"He's going to grow up to see that his family turned his back on him. How do you think that makes him feel? Or me?"

"He will grow up and realize how irresponsible he was."

"No, he will just learn that he wasn't good enough for you."

"Do you think I like it any better than you do? How do you think *I* feel? You're not the only one with feelings."

"Honestly, I don't know how you feel, Stephen. All I know is that we go to these events and you come across like a big champion of the faith but I look at you and think you're full of shit. You can't even see to the support and education of your son but you have no problem arguing that other kids in our parish do. The reality is that St. Benedict's needs to have places like Fr. Bao is fighting for, fighting people like you so that others have some place to come where they can be accepted for who they are, without judgment. For people like our son. For our own son!"

She turned angrily, letting her words hang. There would be no more conversation. The airily light jazz tune awkwardly filling the space that separated them, adding to the already widening gulf.

Stephen turned left at East 27 Avenue and as they drove slowly down their own street, both of their eyes fell upon familiar houses that tenuously tied them to a shared past like a row of memories on a quickly unraveling string. They saw the homes where Rebecca and Michael played with their friends after school, the ones where they met the kids' parents for the first time and eventually became friends themselves. Some parents they remained close to, others either moved or drifted away as each of their kids made new friends outside the neighbourhood. They saw the row of houses that Michael played road hockey in front of, well into June sometimes during NHL playoffs. Or the family homes that Rebecca stayed over for pajama parties, where later she kissed her first boy, and even tried smoking pot. They knew this to be true as Michael found her diary one day and tormented her older sister by threatening to tell on her, which he ended up blurting out over dinner anyways.

And then there was the house Stephen was called to walk Michael home from because he was too drunk to stand and his clothes were mostly missing. He always seemed to experiment with clothes, going out wearing one outfit, coming home with something else. Marie and Stephen also saw the house where Rebecca and her friends planned their grad party and later, her university courses before she and her friend left to stay in residence in Victoria.

Finally rounding the corner along the Renfrew Ravine Park, they automatically looked at the grey stucco house that Michael was kicked out from last year, vowing never to come back. The house held the most distant memories, clouded now by the dull ache of regret. Where brother and sister once lived together but only daughter came to visit now. The home where Stephen began to qualify his love for his son, which of course he still denies. Marie knew otherwise, as did their children.

Not having Michael around made it easier to pretend he loved his son the same, without being reminded every day of his orientation. Stephen tried to accept him as a teen, at first talking to Marie about what he heard Michael say, or how he said it. Marie reassured Stephen, saying it was just a phase and not to worry about it. But then the clothing became more bizarre and friends more blatantly gay, which made it harder to dismiss their son's new-found identity as mere experimentation.

When they were little, Stephen taught both his son and daughter to be strong, and to express their opinions confidently. To assert themselves. So when Michael finally did assert himself, telling his parents following the party he had at the house while they were away, and boldly introduced his boyfriend as had been taught to do, Stephen chose to take it all back. His teachings, his support, his love. His son flaunted his identity like a slap across Stephen's face.

Even when a father's anger and hurt resides, as it often does with time, Stephen remained embarrassed of his son. He grew more emotionally distant and ashamed of his son's behaviour, relying on Marie to be the go-between. Instead of asking Michael to do something, he would just get Marie to tell him, which she resented.

Ultimately, Stephen blamed Marie, taking out his frustration on her. The way he saw it, she kept encouraging him and accepting his behaviour. Michael could tell his Dad had completely withdrawn, especially compared with how easy it appeared Stephen was able to laugh and talk with Rebecca. Michael felt different, not that he believed he was, but by how he was ignored and made invisible in his father's eyes. Marie always believed in her heart that Michael took the money from his parents just to be noticed, not to drive a further wedge between him and his father.

Stephen and Marie pulled into the driveway of the grey stucco house as the sun lowered in the sky, bathing the westward view of their home in fading red light. The two-story house looked stately, standing tall before the ravine on the opposite side of the street. Michael and Rebecca played in the ravine when they were young, going on walks with their dad and engaging in imaginary games of explorers, or scaring themselves that a bear may be around the corner of the trail. Before they emerged from the ravine after a long walk, they would see their house from below, peering above the ferns and cedars, welcoming them back.

Now it seemed the ravine pulled the parents deeper into hurt and resentment, like a magnet, without providing a way back. Although the children left home and reached for something new in their lives to make their own way forward, Stephen and Marie wandered still in a ravine of their own making. It was the sadness of their parent's lives that made going home to visit unbearable. Rebecca felt obligated and dutifully visited regularly for Sunday dinner when she could. Michael could never visit for fear of being compromised further, either by his father's disapproving looks, or his mother's guilt. Rebecca shared common roots with Michael, but the younger brother would no longer be defined by it.

Stephen put the car in park, pausing before turning the engine off. In silence, they got out of the car, walked up to the sidewalk to the front door, and entered one after another into the lonely ravine they called home.

CHAPTER 12

Hesitantly, Magda touched Babcia's arm as they were alone in the kitchen putting away the last of the Sunday dishes. The other women were busy relaxing outside, cooling themselves under the birch trees at the edge of the yard while the young children played. Together, their laughter and animated conversation drifted through the kitchen window, muting the deep voices of the men in the adjacent parlour down the hall as they sipped cognac and smoked rolled cigarettes.

Babcia frowned in reaction to Magda's touch, as if to say, 'We have work to do, granddaughter, and this is no time to stop while there are still chores.' Babcia had already sent Magda's mother and aunts outside so she could tidy up her own kitchen after all the women washed and dried the dishes. This was a task she left for Magda and herself to do, without having to endure further unnecessary chatter, especially given it was still hot in the kitchen. Babcia was reserved and observant, feeling no need to talk unless it was necessary. But despite her detached nature, she secretly enjoyed her granddaughter's company. Magda was quiet like herself and did not carry on like the other fools. She directed Magda to put the serving plate on the shelf that was beyond her reach, but Magda did not move. She held the plate in her hands, shielding her body.

"Babcia?" she said timidly. Babcia carried on without looking, still frowning, avoiding her granddaughter's attempt to engage in conversation. Magda rested her hand on her grandmother's arm.

Finally, the old woman spoke.

"You are so tall, Magda, how would we eat without you? We would all have to use our kitchen aprons and buttoned coats if not for your long arms to reach Babcia's fine china."

Magda managed a brief smile before it dropped instantly when she heard one of the men get up from the parlour, walking down the hallway on the creaky wooden floor towards the washroom, closing the door noisily behind him and locking it. Magda's hand tightened on her grandmother's weathered arm, but Babcia pulled away to sort the remaining silverware and put it in the little felt box on the kitchen counter, still frowning as she did so.

"Babcia? I have to tell you something." She looked anxiously at Babcia's busy hands that never ceased moving.

"Babcia, please stop what you are doing."

Babcia's frown dropped slowly, becoming an absent stare. She did not look up, continuing to put aside the remaining everyday cutlery in a separate cupboard drawer.

Magda pressed on in a hushed voice, first looking down the hallway before bringing her face to Babcia's ear, desperation growing each moment they remained alone in the kitchen.

"I know you know, Babcia, but I do not understand why you have never said anything. Even now you remain silent."

Babcia fumbled slowly with the last of the ordinary utensils, staring into the drawer.

"Why, Babcia, how could you not protect me?"

She placed her hand on her grandmother's own pair of tireless, weathered hands, stopping the utensils from clanging. Babcia panted in slow heavy breaths, like a series of sighs.

"Why?" Magda whispered again as tears fell down her face. She no longer cared about the men in the parlour, or the other women and children in the yard. She learned to distance herself from her father's voice. Each time it happened, he disappeared further from mind. She endured his forcible entry only to guarantee his complete and irrevocable severance from her life. Her mother's betrayal hurt worse, and she hated her all the more for it. Magda tried telling her mother once to make him stop but she only blamed Magda for the husband's actions, which she saw as favouring daughter over mother. She blamed Babcia too for raising him and permitting their marriage. Magda knew her father hurt her mother as well, but as long as there was someone else to deflect the pain, her mother said nothing to Magda. For her mother to admit it would be to accept some degree of blame. She would not have this conversation with her daughter again.

Magda wanted to scream at her mother and make her say something, to rip her voice from her throat just to get some response, but nothing ever came to pass. In time, Magda stopped expecting anything from her parents other than betrayal. She only listened to Babcia's voice now, and barely she ever spoke.

Babcia turned slowly, taking hold of Magda's hands before looking up to meet her thirteen-year-old granddaughter's pleading eyes in her own.

"I am an old woman, and my memories are faded. Today is enough to worry about."

Confused, Magda began to speak, a thousand questions racing through her head. Before words could be formulated, Babcia added,

"You can reach to put away Babcia's dishes that I can no longer do. You can reach for more than an old bent over woman can ever give you."

She held Magda's hands, squeezing them gently. Magda felt both their fragility and warmth.

Magda looked through the kitchen window out onto the yard where her mother laughed with her aunts, sipping their fruit drinks and fanning themselves in the shade under the trees.

"You know, Babcia, I can't talk to her. Without you I have no one."

Babcia smiled, full of affection and pride.

"Without you, Granddaughter, to reach up for my dishes and to help an old woman believe she is not too much of a burden, I have no one, either."

Magda pulled her grandmother close and held her, feeling the bones along her spine and the tremor of her body as she was lifted upward slightly by Magda's embrace.

An eruption of laughter from the men in the parlour interrupted their embrace. Magda backed away abruptly.

"But what am I to do? I cannot stay at my house any longer."

Babcia stiffened, her frown returning. She spoke sternly.

"Your place is at home. It is not for us to decide."

"No, I can't, Babcia. How can you even say that?"

"You must listen to me, Magda, and know there is a way for us that is not always ours to decide. You have to think of the family, for that is all we have. That is what keeps us strong, to endure despite the many wars and hardships our country has known."

"No, Babcia. We are not strong if we lie to ourselves and suffer in silence."

"It is the way for our kind. You must accept this."

Magda began to cry loudly.

"Stop this silliness!" Babcia said harshly.

Magda looked at her grandmother with disbelief, stepping back further. Babcia turned slowly again towards the counter, returning to her task of sorting the fine utensils into the felt silverware box and the others into the cupboard drawer, making sure everything was in its place. Magda continued to sob. Annoyed, Babcia picked up another serving plate from the table and placed it firmly into Magda's hands. Pushing away her own conflicted feelings for which she had no words.

"Now, Magda, stop being a silly child and put this away for Babcia."

Magda held the plate in her hands dejectedly, looking at her grandmother as if seeing for the first time her weakness and her own secrets. A secret no doubt shared by her mother, her aunts, and maybe by one of the other children in the yard, under disguise of laughter and cognac. An accomplice for the sake of keeping the family together.

Magda put the plate back on the counter and walked out of the room, past the parlour and cigarette smoke and Babcia's yard, past all she ever knew and endured. She could no longer stay if even Babcia remained silent.

Yet, Babcia did speak, which Magda only remembered and finally understood the night she got up from her seat on the SkyTrain with her baby she bore in secret. Babcia called to her granddaughter, encouraging her to reach for something more.

Babcia looked up as her granddaughter left the kitchen, and then slowly back at the serving plate left behind on the counter. She took it and wrapped it in her tea towel that she was using to dry the utensils, folding the corners over the plate carefully as her hands shook. Babcia raised it slowly over her breast, too short to put it away, feeling the full weight of the burden she carried.

CHAPTER 13

Sandy and Tanis met Fr. Bao in the sacristy, where he had gone after he said goodbye to the committee members following the retreat to prepare for the afternoon Mass. Other volunteers were beginning to gather including the servers, readers and an altar boy, who was more a late teen than a boy. Sandy kept his voice low but his tone was direct.

"Why didn't you tell us about Mai Ly?"

"I didn't see any reason to. What connection does my knowing her have to the person who left her baby?"

"The woman, I would add, who is now dead. Her name was Magda and she was wearing your friend's coat. What exactly is the nature of your relationship with Mai Ly?"

Fr. Bao stared at Sandy, disregarding the question and the awkward presence of the others in the sacristy.

"Listen, if you think I have anything to do with the woman who died other than what I told you, then say so, but spare the innuendo tactics."

Tanis looked at Sandy then back to Fr. Bao. The volunteers hurried what they were doing and went into the church to finish their preparations, leaving the three of them alone in the sacristy.

Sandy apologized. "Sorry, Father. I meant no disrespect. What I'm asking is if you have any idea how Mai Ly is connected to Magda. Was there anything she may have said about her background? About her family for example, or people she knew?"

"I never heard her mention Magda by name but she did talk about a new girl who she was looking out for. I gathered she was not used to the scene."

"You seem pretty used to the scene yourself for a priest." Sandy couldn't resist pointing it out. Fr. Bao glared at him.

Tanis added, "Fr. Bao. Do you recognize this?" She showed him the silk scarf sealed in a small clear plastic bag. "I believe you gave this to Mai Ly."

Fr. Bao took the bag, holding it reverently in his hand, turning it over slowly. The tightness in his face dropped.

Tanis added. "We found it on the young woman. Is it yours?"

He didn't answer.

"Father?"

"It's my sister's. He handed the plastic bag back to Tanis.

"The initials," Sandy asked, "are they your sister's?"

"Yes, A'nh," he said flatly. The cruel irony of the plastic bag was readily apparent. Her memory had become increasingly opaque like the seal around the keepsake.

"Does she live here in Vancouver?" Sandy pursued further.

"No, we don't know where she is. I haven't seen her since we came over."

"From Vietnam?" Tanis asked. She previously worked in the City of Vancouver's New Immigrants program and knew what the boat people endured following the end of the war.

"Yes, twenty-three years ago now," he confirmed vacantly.

"Is that what brings you to the Eastside, Father?" Tanis added, understanding. "To try to find your sister?"

"Perhaps."

"Perhaps yes or perhaps no?" Sandy pushed.

Fr. Bao didn't reply. He turned mechanically to the large lectionary book open on the sacristy counter to mark the readings for Mass with one of the book's ribbons.

"Can I ask you why you gave A'nh's scarf to Mai Ly?" Tanis asked.

"Probably the same reason Mai Ly gave it to the woman. For hope. We all have to hang onto something, Officers."

"Even after twenty-three years?" Tanis said softly, more a statement than a question. She thought of her own father, wishing she still had something tangible to hold onto. A seal more opaque than plastic had shrouded her own cherished memories.

"Yes, even after all the years. Now, unless you have other questions, I have to get ready for Mass."

"Of course, Father," Sandy offered respectfully. "I'm sorry we have to ask you all these questions. We're just doing our jobs."

"I understand, and I'm doing my own."

"As a priest, or a brother?" Tanis asked compassionately.

"Both, I suppose, but right now people are gathering and parishioners can be even more demanding than the police, if you know what I mean."

"I do, Father," said Sandy. "I go to the eight-thirty on Sunday mornings at Our Lady of the Assumption in Port Coquitlam."

"Yes, that's wonderful. If I may?"

"Thank you, Fr. Bao. Oh, and the scarf, we will see that you get this back when the investigation is concluded. If there is a trial we may need it longer, but for now we'll hold onto it."

"It's okay. It's time to let it go."

"The scarf, or the memory of your sister?" asked Sandy.

Again, Fr. Bao did not answer. He looked away, taking the lectionary book in his hands to bring it into the church. Sandy looked at Tanis, shrugged, then together they left. It was the last time they talked to Fr. Bao.

After dropping Tanis off at the care centre so she could feed her dad supper, Sandy eagerly drove home, looking forward to time with Allison and the kids. It wasn't too late to go to the garden centre and still have a barbeque. He could even save a step and pick up the soil and peat moss on his way home.

Sandy thought of the scarf that bound Fr. Bao and his sister over the years, imaging what would bind him to his own family if ever he was

separated from them. The silk threads of his marriage were already beginning to unravel one at a time, and he knew he couldn't afford to ignore
their relationship anymore.

He remembered his promise earlier that day, smiling as he turned onto
the eastbound lane of Highway 1 for Port Coquitlam.

CHAPTER 14

On another evening years ago, Allison remembered Sandy coming in the door, not sure what to expect. She never knew what frame of mind he'd be in. When they were first married, they had energy in the evening when he came home, to talk, to make love, to talk some more afterwards. In the stillness of the night, they shared their vulnerabilities, trusting they were each other's best friend and were secure in their love.

For Allison, she needed to know she was enough. That she was smart enough. That she was respected at work for who she was besides her good looks. She wanted to know if Sandy saw her too. That she was not just the wife he so jealously guarded. That she was not invisible.

Allison often asked herself if Sandy took her for granted. In fact, he nearly got into a fight with another man who was flirting with her at a party before she was really sure he still cared. They were both falling into the insidious trap of an easy, comfortable marriage that afforded no surprises. Later he blamed her for encouraging the flirt.

It was through that subsequent argument that she realized how lonely she was. The loneliness grew more pronounced with Sandy's obsession at work and the times he remained a cop long after he came home. It was rare now, but when he held her after passionately making love, once his heavy breathing and elevated heart rate stilled, he would talk in guarded murmurs about the fears that drove him. The demons in his life that demanded more of him, in which Sandy, like Allison, felt he never measured up. He talked about his genuine longing to right the wrongs of injustice in which innocent people suffered, failing to recognize that the beautiful woman in his arms also needed his attention, and was crying out to be seen and heard.

She listened, of course, as a dutiful wife would, and Sandy loved her for that, vowing to protect her even more. But the spirit inside Allison that needed expression felt the confines of this protection like a prison. She was grateful then for gardening to set her free. Only then did she find moments to tend to the fragile and tender plants that personified her life.

As Sandy came home that evening seven years ago, she teetered on the edge. Learning that she was pregnant with Timmy evoked so many mixed emotions. Although it was planned, it was not until her doctor confirmed the pregnancy that she realized just how unprepared she was for parenthood. A week had since passed.

She was not prepared to tell Sandy until she had time to sit with her own questions. She wondered if the experience of giving birth and bringing new life in the world would satisfy her own longing to be fulfilled, to be more than she saw herself to be, or whether it would just substitute one role for another. At least as wife she had time apart from Sandy in her work at the lab to claim her own identity, without being ignored one moment by his work obsessions or smothered by a rage of jealousy in another. Now as both a wife and mother, was there going to be anything left over for herself?

Allison thought of the man at the party often, and what it felt like to be pursued, to be desired. Even though she knew it was an illusion, such affairs of the imagination kept her from ever forgetting she would allow herself to be defined simply by a role. She had worked too hard and had too many arguments with Sandy to get him to trust her. Convincing him that he didn't need to protect her. To trust her that despite what he saw on the streets every day, the world was still meaningful and worthy of hope, at least in the promise of their marriage.

Without being a protector then, Sandy asked, who was he? His own dad was controlling, deciding what was needed for the family and for his mom especially, modeling for Sandy of what constituted his proper role. Allison confronted Sandy long before they got married, declaring she would leave him right then if he ever dared tried to make decisions for her like his dad did for his mom. That was not how Allison's parents treated one another, which was her point of reference. So instead of trying to control her life, he poured himself into work, attempting to reverse the wrongs suffered by those lacking Allison's tenacity to push back.

Inevitably, he learned that there was not enough of him and far too many needs for him to ever succeed, which explained his frequent irritability and general unhappiness. In light of his struggles at work, Allison asked herself, would Sandy be more inclined to control their family once he learned of her pregnancy, finding a new way to channel his compulsions?

Allison feared for her unborn child, wondering in time if their child would have her courage to push back, to remind his or her father that the world is good and he could still trust. She knew all too well what was at stake, and in a moment, so would Sandy. All what they had accomplished and struggled in their relationship seemed at risk of unraveling simply with the words, "I'm pregnant."

Allison stood in the kitchen as Sandy came in through the garage door. She heard his car pull in and put down the tea towel and cup she was drying. She couldn't be sure she was ready to tell him but knew he deserved to know. Her right hand slid over her belly, drawing courage for both of them. She imagined there would be many times in the future that she may need to speak up for their children's interests, and this first occasion gave her confidence she would always do so. She was already a mother, and she hoped Sandy would claim the gift of fatherhood too. She grew excited for this possibility, and for Sandy. Despite his misguided intentions, she saw the goodness of his heart that would serve to protect her baby, and her, always.

Once he came in and she told him, there was no longer any reason to stop believing in that possibility. His momentary disbelief was expected, as was his strong, reassuring embrace. She in turn assured him it was okay to make love to celebrate their news. Through the walls of the house afterwards their soft murmurings sounded, the same comforting sounds their children would hear later when waking up in the middle of the night when little bladders filled. The murmurings that would allow the children to fall back asleep, feeling warm and secure.

Tonight, Allison and Sandy did not talk long afterwards as they did in the past. Allison was tired. Despite her previous protests, she was surprised how much she needed his protection, burying herself in his arms. Rather than losing herself, she discovered something new within, beyond her identity either as parent or as spouse, which she was beginning to relish. It took her uttering those two words to make it real.

It would not be the same for Sandy, however. Not until Timmy's precocious spirit and Nicole's innocence called out to him later did he fully believe in the possibility that Allison came to know for certainty that night seven years ago. She would always have this physical connection to the children and the strength of her beliefs to hold onto this possibility when she knew, invariably, Sandy would falter. Before sleep overtook her, she thought of her garden. Lying with her head on Sandy's chest, she remembered that her garden never failed to flourish and come into bloom, despite hail or frost. She had to believe this, for all of them.

CHAPTER 15

Later Saturday evening, Fr. Bao poured himself a Scotch, grateful the day was finally over, and that he still had time alone in the rectory before Fr. Andrew returned tomorrow. He turned on Hockey Night in Canada featuring the late game between the Edmonton Oilers and the Calgary Flames in Edmonton, which normally would be of interest as playoffs approached and the significance of the outcome for the Canucks' overall standings. But he was restless and paced the room, looking outside. Thinking of her.

Thinking of whom, precisely? Certainly A'nh, upon seeing her scarf again. He gave it to Mai Ly believing he had finally accepted that his sister was gone, convincing himself that it was time to move on, only to be surprised that it would return to him a few weeks later through Magda's tragic circumstances. My God, he realized, she would have had it with her in the confessional last night.

There always seemed some tenuous link to his sister, even when he tried to forget. At first, he clung to the hope she was in Thailand, as the villagers in the boat insisted. When he naively traveled to Thailand ten years later in search of her when he became an adult, bringing with him her scarf and a worn picture from their early childhood years in Vietnam, he was overwhelmed, not knowing where to begin. The sex trade market was everywhere, only adding to his despair. He limited his search where it was known Vietnamese girls taken from the boats were sold, passing her picture around to anyone who bothered to look.

Of course, no one recognized her, or if they thought they did, he was told many different variations of where she purportedly lived, or what name she now went under, or who she married, and ultimately, what became of her. After a young Thai boy, who insisted he knew her, took the picture to ask his friends where she lived but never came back, Bao went home with only her one remaining keepsake.

He also thought of Mai Ly tonight. He did not tell the police how he came to know her, and he was glad they didn't persist with their questions. He stopped looking after Thailand and the repeated futile inquiries with the Canadian embassies throughout Southeast Asia, with immigration authorities in Ottawa, and his one and probably only visit back to Vietnam a few years ago. It was too hard to have his expectations continuously raised only to be dashed when another lead turned up empty. Until he met Mai Ly.

A random conversation with her as he walked to the SkyTrain station on a street in Chinatown after a conference changed that. It was more than her resemblance to A'nh but the fact she approached Fr. Bao that mattered. That she reached out and found *him*, not realizing until that moment how lost he had become. Even in trying to hustle him, he felt she knew him. She obviously singled him out for reasons unknown to her. But he knew differently.

He believed she needed him and all that he represented with his white collar and calming presence. That he was strong and noble, as his mother said. He knew she was searching for a way out and he could help her. He could make her whole, and by letting him help her, it could take away his own emptiness.

At first, it was providing her money for coffee and food, then a bus ticket to make her escape to some fictitious home that ended up her nose instead. He learned he had to be more direct, actually taking her somewhere to eat, paying for her time to give her pimp so they could have coffee and talk while getting out from the cold rain. He brought her warm clothes and shampoo. He provided medication samples for her and all the women she worked with that he got from his physician friend Tom. Some of the clothes he bought her were not worn long, no doubt in exchange for more drugs, but at least it served as an excuse to visit her on the street again and take her shopping.

For Christmas last year, he accompanied her to get her hair and nails done as a way of doing something special for her. To make her feel special. As she was transformed in the salon, he saw A'nh's image emerging before him. He no longer needed the picture that was stolen to keep her sister's memory alive. He had Mai Ly.

He committed to do more work on behalf of the outreach ministry group in the Eastside, justifying more trips downtown to see her. She was not always on the street when he came by, and so when days would go by that he didn't see her, Fr. Bao worried. He would tell her that when they met up later, pleading she call if she was ever in trouble or needed anything. At first she was flattered by his concern, but soon found it stifling. She started to avoid him, working on different streets further from the Stadium-Chinatown SkyTrain station. One time when they were eating lunch in an Eastside diner, she stole money from his wallet in his coat when he went to use the washroom. He discovered that later in the evening when he got home, but said nothing for fear of losing her. She kept testing him by telling him stories of her work to shock him, to repulse him and make him go away, but still he came back.

Sometimes they talked of the Vietnam that she never knew, born only after her parents left the country following the war. She did not speak of her parents or sisters very often, but he saw how she reacted when he asked about them, changing the subject in a casual way as if she was hiding something. Perhaps guilt, Fr. Bao thought. However, when he asked about boyfriends, she did not hide her feelings of anger. She had little respect for men, especially the men who used women and provided for her livelihood. It was the only work she knew, and even the priest who visited her paid for her time in one way or another. She saw Fr. Bao was getting something out of their time together so she didn't feel guilty, even though she was stringing him along.

One afternoon when Mai Ly was upset and angry about a bad date, he gave her the silk scarf and told her to keep it. She knew it belonged to his sister and didn't really want it. She resented being tied to it, to be indebted to him. When he insisted, Mai Ly took it and gave it that night to Magda, the new girl who didn't use anyone for her own purposes as all the others did.

Yes, he admitted in seeing the silk scarf again, it was really Mai Ly who dominated his thoughts. He feared for her and what all the women like Magda and A'nh endured. He was angry at the decision at the retreat today and the apathy he saw in people who didn't at least try to make a difference, as flawed and apparently wounded as they all were. His mind was racing and could not stop obsessing of dark, foreboding thoughts. He drank back his glass of Scotch, reached for his jacket and car keys, and left.

CHAPTER 16

Luc stood pissing in the toilet, spitting as he did so. He was still tired and hung over from the night before. He opened several cupboard drawers, slamming them loudly before he found some Tylenol. He glanced outside the bathroom window and saw it was getting dark and time to get going, which he resented, given how he felt. It was more than resentment, actually. More an overarching sense of hatred. Hatred for the women he owned. Hatred for the people who paid to use their services. Hatred for being inconvenienced, as he was in having to go out tonight in the rain.

He took several Tylenol, drinking sideways from the bathroom faucet to wash it down and get the bloody taste out of his mouth, wincing as he did so from the bright red sores in the back of his throat. He hated weakness, too. In himself, and in others. It was weakness telegraphed on his face that gave license to his mother's boyfriends and the other men she brought home to beat him when he was little. Luc had no respect for his mother, who did nothing to protect him while he cowered in the corner getting beaten week after week. At times, she even asked the boyfriends to hit Luc for her when she was tired of slapping him around herself.

Luc learned to show his anger at all times and fight back, pushing down any signs of weakness so as not to be a victim. Pushing down the pain in his throat. He learned the power of hatred. Instead, he harnessed pure, unadulterated rage that magnified his strength so he was able to punch and kick and bite or do whatever it took to let her mother's boyfriends know they were no longer welcome and to get the hell out. Until one day when he decided he was tired of fighting for the rights of his mother's place when what he really wanted was his own to defend, his own life to rule. Luc's mother learned the same lesson too, until one day someone angrier than her broke her neck. That was long after Luc left home to fend for himself, and he couldn't care less when his aunt told him what happened. With this in mind, he obviously could not let his sore cancerous throat provide others the upper hand tonight. He would never let anyone know he was hurting. He spit more of the bloody taste into the dirty sink.

Besides weakness in others, he hated people who thought they were smarter than him. Clever people who used clever words as a way of deflecting his threats. Rather than standing up to fight with their fists, they lorded their smugness, which Luc interpreted as another variation of making people cower in the corner as their inferior, like her mother's boyfriends treated him previously.

He taught the women whose interests he protected that it was best to just fear him, not to challenge him or to show weakness, but just do as they were told. To make him money and not give him any trouble. Every day he had to make his rounds to see if his girls were making him money and not causing him any grief. He wished he could trust them, but he couldn't. He couldn't trust anyone. Today was a case in point; he had to teach one particular individual a lesson, and tomorrow it would be another. He put on his pants and did up his shirt and jacket, spitting again in the sink before going outside into the night.

Later that month from his hospital bed, the nursing staff would say he even looked angry while unconscious. The sores in the back of his mouth were biopsied for oral cancer, further aggravated by the endotracheal tube that was inserted temporarily to help him breathe until a permanent tracheotomy could be performed for long-term ventilation. Some staff found it difficult caring for him given his history, but were obligated to treat him with respect, as due any patient. After all, he was a human being, was he not?

Certainly, he was not always this way. At what point in his abusive childhood did something shift that would change how people saw him? When it was no longer required to feel sorry for him, and instead to begin fearing him?

His aunt never feared him even when Luc pushed her away after his mother's death. She had always tried to look out for Luc, especially because her nephew grew up with a lot of different men in his mother's life, but no real father figure to mentor the boy. When he was a baby, with a full head of dark hair, ruddy complexion and high cheek bones, his aunt stepped in to look after Luc when his mother went on a drunken binge with her latest boyfriend. His aunt sang to him and rocked him, but when his mother reappeared a few days later and saw them bonding, she became jealous and took the baby from her sister's arms, telling her to get out. Luc's aunt knew it was an act and as soon as she walked out her door, the baby would be left to cry in his cradle as usual.

After a few months, Luc's aunt noticed the baby didn't cry as much anymore, and was agitated when he she tried to hold him. That was when she first noticed the bruising. During those days when Luc's mother was away drinking, his aunt was tempted to take him with her and leave for good, but she was afraid of her sister and her threats of what she or her boyfriends would do to her. It was obvious Luc's mother resented the baby but at the same time refused to let anyone take him off her hands.

Even when her boyfriends complained about Luc, who had now become a toddler, she made sure the boy stayed with her. He belonged to her and it was her decision how he should be raised, even if she resented his presence. Luc grew up knowing his mother cared just enough to see that he wasn't taken away, meaning the bruises were hidden from view and the monthly child support cheques kept coming in. She also saw that he had a good meal from time to time so he slept well without bothering her, assuming there was still money left over after she went partying.

When Luc was old enough, she made sure he went to school to get a break from him during the day, but basically nothing changed. She remained emotionally detached. When he acted up, she found it easier to get her boyfriends to physically discipline him, as he responded to their belts more. Besides, Luc was bigger by the time he went to school. When she did hit him, it was usually when she was in a drunken rage.

But not every boyfriend was physically abusive. In fact, one man she stayed with a long time never laid a hand on him or his mother. Instead, he had a sarcastic tongue and could belittle both of them by pointing out their flaws, making them feel inferior and insignificant. He would call the boy useless and stupid, predicting he would never amount to much. And the mother was simply a bitch and a whore. Of all the boyfriends, and there were many, Luc hated him the most. He must have finally got bored or found someone else to belittle because one day he never came back. It was the only boyfriend Luc's mother didn't have to throw out herself.

Throughout these years, Luc's aunt tried to maintain some relationship with him, careful not to interfere and provoke her sister's anger. While she tried to intervene when she could, and provide some parenting tips when her sister was receptive, in Luc's mind his aunt was just as useless as his mother. Luc didn't know about her efforts to have him apprehended by the Quebec social service agencies and placed in her care, or at least in a foster care agency. He only knew his mother resented his aunt and that like his mother, his aunt made promises that she couldn't keep. It really made no difference to him as nothing changed in the end. He couldn't count on anyone but himself. It was up to him to survive his mother's binge drinking and neglect, her boyfriends who routinely beat him, and an aunt who said she cared and would take him away but who also didn't keep her promise.

Once he started attending school, he saw how different he was than the other boys. He assumed it was expected to be smacked around by people bigger than him or belittled by adults, and that feeling angry all the time was normal. He viewed the other kids as placid and weak, especially if they cowered when he threatened them and made them do his bidding. He found it easy to intimidate his classmates, even ones bigger than him, just by staring them in the face and using his angry voice to force the other kids to back down. If they didn't back down, he would use his fists and that usually got them to do what he wanted. When his mother made him go to school on an empty stomach, he would just take food from another kid or steal their lunch money, or both. The more he was beaten up or mocked at home, the more he needed some release for his rage at school. If he was sent home for fighting, his mother would yell at him for being so difficult, and then the boyfriends would slap Luc and tell him to smarten up, only reinforcing the cycle.

His mother couldn't cope with his increasingly disruptive behaviour and withdrew further from him, finding her own escape in the bottle. Although she would have never admitted it, as Luc became bigger and meaner, she began to fear him, keeping the boyfriends around to help manage him, even if she resented them as well. Instinctively she sought out tougher men to bring into her life, which meant Luc's beatings became more severe, and correspondingly caused more violent fights at school to release his pent-up rage. Calls from concerned teachers led his mother to drink more to avoid having to think about it, hence further beatings or belittling, until finally Luc had enough. He moved out, leaving his mother to fend for herself from the violent men in her life she increasingly surrounded herself with. Without Luc as a convenient target, the men turned to his mother to vent their own anger and frustration. Luc actually laughed when his aunt told him someone broke his mother's neck, saying she got what she deserved. He just wanted to know if she left him any money.

As this violent history began getting pieced together later by the hospital social workers at St. Paul's Hospital, it created conflict among some of the other members of the care team looking after him. It was easier turning him in bed and bathing him without knowing all this about his childhood past. The police presence at the hospital was a constant reminder of his known criminal background but only a few sketchy hints of the violence he was subjected to growing up provided a counter perspective to garner any sympathy. Some of the people who visited Luc, including the sex trade workers who feared him and wanted it be known on record they came by to see him in hospital, perpetuated the unconscious prejudice of the staff towards their patient. They knew if he could only wake up and speak, they would feel better as they suspected it probably wouldn't take long to see his personality coming through to justify their aversion towards him. As long as Luc lay in this in-between state, it was hard to know exactly what to think or feel towards him.

It was a very different experience on the previous Saturday night when Luc angrily descended the stairs of his apartment with the taste of blood in his mouth, spitting as he went. When he did the rounds among his women on the streets, it was abundantly clear what others thought and felt about him.

CHAPTER 17

From the mist shrouded sidewalk, Mai Ly peered furtively into the store front window, pretending she was getting something from her purse. She was conscious of how ostentatious she dressed and what her presence would have appeared to those walking by. Who was she to pretend being worthy of such elegance? Still, she often imagined herself wearing one of the long brightly-coloured gowns hanging on the racks running the length of the rectangular shaped wood panel store in Chinatown. The fabrics were magnificently warm and inviting under the incandescent lights, in stark contrast to the wet cigarette stained sidewalk where Mai Ly stood. Often on her way to and from work, she would pause outside the store, carrying on with the charade that she needed something from her purse, or to adjust her shoe, or to look at the paper she carried in her hand as though it were today's fashion shopping list.

She never stopped for long, just enough to glance in at the mannequins wearing the traditional Vietnamese áo dài in an array of festive reds, aqua blues and sunshine yellow fabrics. There was even a mannequin adorned in a beautiful white áo dài with a matching cylinder shaped nón lá hat, evoking memories of the family wedding she attended years ago in Montréal when she was eleven. Her mother and older sisters wore the traditional dress, and Mai Ly was upset that she couldn't as well. Her mother explained they did not have the money, which her gangly and flat chested daughter interpreted to mean she was not beautiful enough like her sisters. Mai Ly did not understand the humiliation her mother endured just to borrow a few dresses from friends for the older girls and her; a humiliation far worse if she went to relatives who already looked down on them. There was no one else her mother could approach who might have a dress for Mai Ly, but of course this was difficult to explain to a pre-teen girl with a temper. Mai Ly was too angry to notice that the dresses disappeared shortly after her cousin's wedding, never to be mentioned again.

It didn't help matters that Mai Ly's two older sisters teased her before the wedding, comparing their eloquent dresses with the hand-me-down she was required to wear. They frequently teased her for several years after whenever Mai Ly asked to borrow their outfits, telling their younger sister that she had no figure. Even if they could be assured Mai Ly wouldn't ruin them through carelessness, they just didn't want her to have them out of spite. This only reinforced to Mai Ly that she was not beautiful enough to wear to wear fine clothes like the áo dài, let alone the cheaper dresses her sisters paid for themselves from earnings garnered by part-time jobs after school or on weekends. Mai Ly wondered if she would ever be pretty like her name meant. Pretty enough that a man would fall in love with her.

With adolescence, Mai Ly rebelled as any other teenager does, but with a fearless and insolent attitude that dared people to deny her what she thought was due her. Whether it was a dress, a privilege to stay out late, or opportunity to experiment with her body as long as there was someone willing to accommodate her wishes. She learned how easy it was to seduce boys and get them to buy her things in exchange for sexual pleasure. At first, it was to get clothes and jewelry to make her look beautiful. Then it was alcohol and pot to experience the thrill of total disregard. She started skipping classes and eventually her grades plummeted, resulting in more arguments with her parents, who tried to ground her, to make her more responsible. She retaliated with more rebellious outbursts and then staying out all night partying. There was a time when Mai Ly envied her older sisters, but now she no longer needed them. She had everything she wanted without having to study or work after school, scrimping and saving to buy clothes that her immigrant parents could never afford.

The sister closest to her age tried to reach out to her, perhaps still guilty for lording their power of rank and privilege over her when they were younger. She pleaded to Mai Ly, saying how important it was to study and to listen to their parents, but to no avail. Mai Ly scoffed at her sister's advice about choosing better friends and heeding the dangers of drugs and promiscuity as prudish. Now it was Mai Ly who felt powerful and grown up. She was different from her sisters in another way. She was able to stand up to their mother, while her sisters were powerless to do so. Their mother did not speak English and her father's proficiency was broken at best, and thus it was expected the girls to speak Vietnamese at home. Mai Ly saw that once her sisters were forced to engage in conversation with their mother, especially in a heated argument, they always acquiesced to their mother's wishes. Stubbornly, Mai Ly knew what her mother said when she scolded her, but instead answered her back in English, pretending she no longer understood Vietnamese. Mai Ly got used to pretending a lot. She saw how pretending got her the things she wanted.

Mai Ly was born in Canada shortly after her family emigrated from Vietnam in 1975, just before the war ended. Her sisters taunted Mai Ly about this too, as they still had memories of life in Vietnam, like the beautiful flowers and lush vegetation. They and their mother always spoke so fondly of it, but Mai Ly obviously didn't know, nor did she care. She hated the stories about Vietnam and said as long as they kept focused on what they lost they would never get ahead. Mai Ly wanted to go forward in life, and to claim what she felt was due her.

During these teen years, Mai Ly's father seemed to withdraw, feeling more inadequate to cope with a rebellious daughter, having learned with Mai Ly's older sisters that he lacked the words and confidence to reach them, even if his English was better. He focused instead on working, struggling with one poor paying job after another, hoping that his children would make it. Unlike Mai Ly, her father felt success would never be within his reach. He grew more sad and helpless. He kept his tears for his beloved third born daughter well hidden. Even after she ran away, he still loved her and prayed for her return. With only infrequent news of her whereabouts and their one failed attempt to bring her home that threatened their lives, he still held out hope in his heart of his daughter's return, which he kept hidden from view. Monetary success was never to be in his grasp, but Mai Ly's return home was always possible to him. This belief was the only thing that kept him from being overcome by despair during the long years of her absence.

By sixteen, Mai Ly knew how to dress for the bars downtown on Crescent Street, doing favours for the bouncers and bartenders who never asked to see her ID. Seedy bars that had plenty of men to buy her drinks or share a line of cocaine in the bathroom in exchange for fellatio. One night a man went too far, tearing at her clothes, which meant more to her than her dignity. She pushed back, screaming at him in the men's bathroom before he hit her in the face, telling her to shut up. Another man walked in the bathroom then and instinctively grabbed her assailant, hitting his head against the bathroom mirror until it broke and was splattered with blood. Her rescuer told Mai Ly to come have a drink with him and they left that bar for another club, not much better than the last. More drinks and cocaine followed, and of course sex in his car, but she didn't care because he was already promising her things, which is all what mattered. He told her his name was Luc, and he had an opportunity for her in which she need not worry about where her next drink or line or meal would come from, if she worked for him. He had friends who would get her fake ID so she could do what she wanted, whenever she wanted.

Even as street wise as Mai Ly, there is still something impressionable about a rebellious sixteen-year-old to latch on to such empty promises. They left that night for Toronto where they lived together for about a year above a strip club. She helped pay the rent by working on the stage below. She saw how men looked at her, desiring her, telling her how beautiful her body was when she lap danced before lusting eyes.

"Look at what the gangly, flat chested girl my sisters teased me about has become now," she thought, happy she left with Luc, even though he was mean and forgot about his promises.

Mai Ly's parents had tracked her down in Toronto, but she refused to go back. They felt defeated, especially when Luc threatened to kill her if they went to police or tried to stop him. As poor immigrants, they felt they had no choice but to go home without their daughter, especially when she rejected their efforts. Luc had plans of making more money with other girls he rescued, who now shared their dungy apartment above the stage, to whom he too promised a better life. By seventeen, Mai Ly was living with him and her new found family of sisters in Vancouver's Eastside, leaving behind a trail of lies and other heartbroken and fearful families equally powerless to stop Luc.

Mai Ly seldom sent a post card or note to her family, even after she became of legal age and was no longer deemed a runaway subject to apprehension by social services. She was still too angry at her parents, blaming them for making her doubt her beauty and powers that she had since discovered and celebrated, despite losing weight and her hair becoming dull and lifeless. As long as she had some liquour and cocaine to keep her pretending, she was fine. Luc had grown meaner and put the girls up in a small one-room apartment, only occasionally giving them what they needed to maintain the lie as long as they were good. And if they listened. He never failed to remind them of his expectations.

Now the choreographed dance was not on a floodlit stage for everyone to see, but on a dungy sidewalk or in shadowy alleyways and parked cars and rooms that were rented by the hour, pre-paid in advance by Luc. When she danced on stage there was always an audience and men would throw money at her, but on the street she had to first hustle and convince wary clients who may be afraid of getting caught that her naked body was worth seeing, and that there was more to experience if they were willing to pay for it.

Initially the chase was exciting, to see how much money she could earn compared to the wages and tips from dancing. The more money she brought in earned Luc's favour, and sometimes he rewarded her with more clothes and nice boots to keep her believing in the promise of an exotic life. Despite the squalor in which she and the other women lived, she did not allow herself to feel any less about her herself. Nor did she feel anything with the men she had sex with, other than the quiet satisfaction of the money she would get. She'd never have to be like her mother, who needed to beg just to borrow to get a cheap wedding dress for the night. Even when Luc took most of the money, she knew it was the power of her body that earned it, and she would always have that power, with or without Luc.

For a while, that was enough, but as Luc became more abusive, forcing her to be with men she despised, it took more to help her pretend. Crack was easier to get and more affordable with the money she skimmed from her earnings, but it was also more powerful. More effective to push back the unpleasant hangover, the pang of hunger in her gut, or the bruising welts from Luc's hand. It was easier to forget while living in a fog, like the mist and darkness in which she was enveloped most nights on the gritty sidewalks of the Eastside.

But when she stood in front of this dress shop and saw the beautiful white áo dài gowns, she could hear echoes of a part of her life that wasn't completely silenced in fog. A life that she knew her parents and sister always held out hope she would return one day. Mai Ly tried to pretend this was not so, but increasingly knew in her heart it was true. Like her cursory glances in the store front window, she could only dare to look briefly at what she left behind out of shame. The brightly coloured dresses were vivid and cheerful, but like the sun would only allow a brief glance for fear of bringing too much of the stark reality of her life into plain view. Likewise, she couldn't afford to look too long if it forced her to make a decision that she was not prepared to make right now. The priest she befriended also tried to shine too bright a light before her. She had to look away and push him back. It was much easier being around the women she lived and worked with. Their light was faded, and the vacant look in their eyes never caused her to look away. Except for Magda. She was the only one.

She remembered seeing her body earlier that day and how beautiful she looked, even in death. There was a presence to Magda, like the warm light and colour reaching out from the dress shop window onto the darkened street to which Mai Ly was still tied. Mai Ly knew the choice to stay with Luc was destroying her life, but she did not know who she was without him. Magda reminded Mai Ly that there was a light within her that had not gone out, and there was still a future worth pursuing.

After Sandy and Tanis dropped her off following the morgue viewing, she went to walk the streets for a while. Her stomach was filled for a change, and surprisingly she had a lot of restless energy. Besides, Luc was still away and she felt free to do as she pleased. She was sad for Magda but also relieved in an odd way. Maybe she was free too. She didn't want this life for Magda, and believed her friend never lost sight of a life beyond the Eastside. She wondered if there would be a funeral for her and who might attend. She knew she had to be there. Maybe the priest would do it, she thought.

It was dusk now, that in-between time that separated the stark light of day in which her life was exposed for all to see, and the darkness when she could blend in with the shadows and be conveniently forgotten. And to forget herself, just doing what needed to be done to get through life. To make the necessary choices to survive. Magda was gone now but Mai Ly would not forget her. She would not be lost among the shadows of figures that come and go on the Eastside, counted only among statistics of missing or murdered women. No one may have actually put their hand on her to account for her death, but who forced her to flee in the first place, to stay hidden in the shadows, to carry her child in secret? Would she not still be here if no one tormented her?

Mai Ly remembered when Magda showed up on the street earlier in the year. From the beginning, Magda had a way of pointing out the disconnection between the choices they both made and their unfulfilled desires to reach for something more. She was obviously scared and naïve, and didn't seem to belong. Her clothes were the first clue. They were way too nice for this neighbourhood if you wanted to show that you belonged. Mai Ly saw her leaning over, talking to a john in his car, whom Mai Ly instinctively knew was going to be bad.

"Hey girl, do you have some lipstick I can borrow?"

Magda turned around to look. The man in the car quickly looked away with a frozen expression. He drove off before Mai Ly could get close to the car.

"Thanks for nothing," said Magda angrily.

"You mean, thanks for everything. Do you know who that was?"

Magda looked at Mai Ly and immediately knew she was a prostitute like her. A prostitute. Magda had difficulty even thinking that word to herself. "What would Babcia think of me?"

"I don't know. Was he a cop?" Magda asked, wanting to know.

"That, girl, was a mean son-of-a-bitch. He beat one of the others girls a little while ago. If Luc saw him he'd drag him out of the car and kick the shit out of him."

"Who's Luc?"

Magda looked with disbelief at the tall woman before her. Mai Ly could not deny that she was beautiful, and there was something more to her. A sadness.

"You're new around here, otherwise you'd know Luc. Where are you from?"

"Around," said Magda vaguely.

"Okay. No big deal. I'm Mai Ly." She stuck out her gloved hand formally. It was cold that evening but thankfully it wasn't raining, making it easier to look into cars before approaching, which was important lately.

"My name is Magda," she replied with equal formality, extenuated by her distinct East European accent. She hesitated, looking warily at Mai Ly before adding, "And yes, I am new."

"New to all this?"

Magda didn't answer. It was obvious to both of them.

"I don't mean to scare you, honey. But in the last year some of the girls have disappeared from the Eastside."

"You mean...?"

"Yes, well, who knows. But you've got to be careful. You shouldn't get too close to the car until you know who you're dealing with. Cops are the least you have to worry about."

"I know that," said Magda defensively.

"That's where Luc comes in. He's a mean bastard but at least you don't have to worry about if you're ever coming home after."

"You're right."

"About what?"

"I'm new here. I don't have a lot of experience."

"You think? If I had your looks, girl, I'd have the world at my feet. C'mon, let's get something to eat. It's friggin cold out anyways. Besides, Luc is probably busy beating up guys like your last would-be customer. He'd be happy for me to bring you home."

"Who says I'm going with anyone?"

"Hey, I just offered to buy you supper, but if you don't want to eat or you already have a place to stay the night, just say so. You look kind of skinny so I advise you not to pass up a free meal when you get a chance. Or free advice."

"I'm sorry. Sure, Mai...?"

"Mai Ly, but everyone calls me Cherry Blossom."

The memory of their first conversation brought back many others in the dungy apartment that Magda did eventually agree to come stay, as well as the advice Mai Ly prided herself in sharing with Magda and the other women. The kind of advice her own sisters failed to provide her when she was young, Mai Ly thought resentfully. Some of the women spoke candidly of their past, including relationships with family, boyfriends, children, even the men like Luc. Others, like Magda, shared little, but they all wore their story on their face nonetheless, which was no less revealing. The men who paid for their services never noticed this muted story. Even if a client looked into any of the women's eyes, it would only happen by accident as they groped feverously and no more than for a fleeting second before looking away in shame. Like the man who panicked and quickly sped away in his car when Mai Ly approached. The only real intimacy the women knew were those occasional times when Luc was gone for a while, providing the safe space to talk among themselves without need for substances to take away the hurt. The rare moments when they allowed themselves to feel and share their pain.

In those first few months, Magda would mostly listen. The sadness on her face intensified if one of the women came back from a bad date and was beaten, or if another spoke of a family member's betrayal, or if someone learned she had HIV. There was poignancy to Magda's sadness that no one dared to name for fear it would expose all of their vulnerability. She was a presence in their lives that everyone knew without saying so. A presence they continued to feel at her sparsely attended memorial service that Sandy Kohler paid for from his own pocket. He was the only man who showed up besides the funeral director. A couple nurses and a volunteer from the hospital who had held Magda's baby attended, as did April from the shelter. Together, only her co-workers, a few people from the hospital and shelter, a police detective, and funeral director were all but the handful who bore testimony to Magda's gift in their lives. Prayers were said for her baby and a card signed that Sandy forwarded onto the social service authorities facilitating the adoption proceedings to give the child when she was older, in hopes one day it would help know something of her mother.

Mai Ly remembered and honoured the baby's mother in her own way as she walked through Chinatown this late afternoon, trying to recall some of the brief conversation of all she knew about her elusive history. She remembered especially the one time when Magda opened up to her only a few weeks ago. It had been raining that night and they were both cold when they came back to their apartment in the early hours of the day before the sun was up. Magda was always wearing sweaters and extra layers of clothing, which didn't help attract clients on the street. It was another thing that communicated she didn't belong. Magda never liked the cold.

"I'm making some tea. Do you want some, Mai Ly?"

"Sure."

The water hissed from the little kettle on their apartment sized stove. Magda washed two cups from the sink and dried them with the tea towel. Reaching for the tea bags on the open shelf above the stove, Babcia's words came back to her, the same words she always thought about and drew comfort from, especially when she was tired and cold. The kettle kept hissing while Magda stood there, holding the little cardboard box of tea in hand with her back to Mai Ly. The sound of the kettle momentarily drowned out the sound of rain against the window pane. Mai Ly was busy changing, taking off her wet clothes and putting on the cheap grey sweat pants and top. They were Luc's gift to her from Stewart's and a symbol of another broken promise. Only because of the persistent high pitched sound of the kettle did she look up and noticed Magda's angular shoulders were shaking.

Mai Ly quickly went over to her, took the still hissing kettle off the stove, turned Magda and pulled her close. The rain re-announced its presence as the kettle quieted and Magda slowly stiffened in Mai Ly's long embrace. Magda never showed her tears. Stepping back from the hug, Magda quickly wiped her eyes with the tea towel, turned off the stove element and mechanically began to pour the tea. How funny, Magda thought, just like Babcia. It was foolish to cry when there was work to be done.

"You don't have to tell me anything, Magda. I won't ever ask you. But know I will always listen."

"I know," said Magda. "Thank you."

They sat down on the small pull-out couch that doubled as Magda's bed, which she shared with another girl who was not back yet. They sipped from their teas, saying nothing. The rain was more audible now, especially with the noise of the occasional car splashing through the puddle on the street below their second floor window.

"I want to thank you for watching out for me. I'm not very good at this."

"You don't have to thank me. You would look out for me too," offered Mai Ly.

"I don't know. I'm not sure I can look out for anyone."

"That's not true," said Mai Ly softly. The feelings of compassion Magda brought

out in her always surprised Mai Ly. Feelings she once knew so deeply for her real family. Mai Ly momentarily asked herself if she didn't belong here, either.

"It is. I thought it once possible. Back home. But not anymore."

"Home. You mean in Poland?" Magda had briefly mentioned where she once lived when Mai Ly inquired about her accent.

"Yes. With Babcia."

"Who's Babcia?"

"She's my grandmother. She was always good to me. She's dead now."

'I'm sorry."

"I'm not. She never said anything. Even when I told her. I couldn't count on my mother, but Babcia, she knew. But she couldn't make it stop."

"Make what stop?" Mai Ly's question trailed off. She didn't want to pry and press for an answer that would confront her of her own past.

"The stuff that brings a girl here. At least me. I don't know about you or the others. But it shouldn't have happened to me. Babcia should have stopped it."

"Could she? Would she even had the power to stop it?" Mai Ly thought of Luc and the power he exerted over her, her parents and sisters when he wouldn't let Mai Ly call them. Who could stop him? He was a monster who would kill her and her family if they tried again to take her back home. Mai Ly felt so guilty for bringing Magda here. Initially it was just to get her warm for a night, then maybe stay a week until she got settled and on her way. But then once the week became a month she eventually belonged to Luc, trapped by the same insidious promises and token gestures of food and shelter as befallen all of them. Mai Ly wondered if it would have been better that Magda got in that car that day and took her chances on her own with strange men lurking in darkened cars than the beast who walked among them, corralling his herd.

"Maybe not, but she could have warned me. At least said something."

"She never said anything?"

"She told me some things, but it was already too late."

"It is never too late, Magda." The more time Mai Ly spent with Magda, the more she remembered better days with her own family. The memories of years ago, when she knew her sisters' love. When they were close, like she felt with Magda this early morning alone in their decrepit apartment. Even when Mai Ly's sisters teased her, she knew deep down her sisters cared.

"It doesn't matter anyways now, 'cause I left. I will never go back. There's nothing there anymore. Once Babcia died, what's the point? Just more men like my father. I took what I needed from them and left."

"When did you come here?"

"In September. Before it got cold. I thought it was going to be warm all year round in Vancouver. Little did I know. Like a lot of things." She drank from her tea with the look of sadness Mai Ly often saw on her face.

"Did you come with anyone?"

"No," Magda shot back angrily.

Mai Ly paused, instinctively looking away. She knew anger must be respected. An emotion she had learned to be wary of which she once perpetuated and fed off when she was an angry teen herself.

Magda appreciated that about Mai Ly. That she didn't judge her. And was always so patient with her, giving her space. She continued, less forcefully.

"I took as much money as I could from the jerk I dumped in Poland and flew on a different round trip ticket to Canada, but I never got on the plane to go back. I lied to him about going to live with him in the States just so he could get me a passport. He had some friends who made me a fake passport and could arrange for another one once we got to the US so we could stay as long as we wanted. For a price of course."

"Of course. Bastards, all of them."

"But I fooled him. Babcia taught me not to waste time with fools. I let him believe I was going with him so he wouldn't suspect, but I left the day before on another airline that he wouldn't know and be able to track me down. I even got rid of the passport so there would be no trail. But not before taking money from him. I did what I needed to do to get away. And if I have to, I will do so again."

"What are you going to do? I know you are not meant for this."

"I don't know. I just need some time. I need money."

"I know someone. Maybe he can help. He is always looking out for me, trying to get me to go back. He can get you to a safe place, without strings attached."

"No," said Magda firmly. "I can't rely on anyone. I got here on my own and I will get out of here. Out of this place. I can't let anything hold me back. Nothing."

It was the one and only time Magda confided in Mai Ly about her past. Mai Ly gave Magda her blue coat that night and told her to keep it, to keep her warm. Joking, Mai Ly told her to use the scarf in the pocket if she was going to cry as it was softer than the dirty tea towel. She told her who gave it to her and where his church was, just off the SkyTrain line, which Fr. Bao himself took for a quick visit to Mai Ly when his absence from the parish wouldn't be noticed. Funny, thought Mai Ly, she never once went to see Fr. Bao, nor did she care. He was Vietnamese like her, and that was about all they had in common. He'd be better off trying to help Magda, she figured. But now, three weeks later, it was too late. Magda was dead, leaving a baby behind.

"A baby? How didn't I know?" thought Mai Ly remorsefully. She asked herself what else she failed to see. In herself. In her family. In Fr. Bao. There was more to her life than this. Like Magda, what hope was she carrying within that she kept hidden from sight? She wondered what would happen to Magda's baby now that she was gone, including the hopes she may have had for her newborn before she died. She recalled how Magda's face looked so serene on the morgue viewing table earlier today. The sadness was finally gone, and for that one small consolation given to her in death, Mai Ly was happy for her.

As Mai Ly walked back to the apartment to rest and change before going back to work, she crossed the street to the bright window that shone so warmly at dusk. But instead of stopping in front of her window as usual and pretending she was looking, she walked right into the store, confidently choosing dresses off the racks to size them against herself in the mirror, and feeling the fabric in her hands. They were wonderfully soft like the scarf she gave to Magda. She felt no shame in being there, asking the shop owners about the materials and where they were made, and telling them about her own Vietnamese wedding dress traditions. As if she had been to many such weddings and owned her own áo dài. She deserved to be there, she thought, just like Magda and all of them deserved to dream and claim a better life.

Once, not very long ago, when Fr. Bao offered to buy her a dress, she purposely led him as far away from this dress shop in Chinatown because she could not bear the shame of standing before a garment that symbolized all what her life wasn't. Mai Ly knew that she needed to claim this experience for herself.

But this afternoon was different. Today, she saw Magda as if for the first time. She was free. And so was Mai Ly.

CHAPTER 18

Stephen sat alone at his desk in the den. Marie had long gone to bed and they barely spoke to one another since they came home from the parish. The den faced the street and was located immediately off the front foyer separated by glass paneled French doors, which was convenient if he had to meet clients at home to provide privacy. It was set up as a satellite office for his law practice and it was not infrequent that he would spend the whole evening after dinner researching and preparing notes for cases. The office was traditionally decorated with a large mahogany desk and burgundy leather button chairs, surrounded by ceiling-high book cases. He was particularly fond of his green shaded desk lamp, which cast a soft, warm light in the room without overpowering the equally lazy amber glow reaching in from the streetlamps outside.

Sometimes Stephen played classical music on the CD player. Tonight, however, he was alone in the quiet of his thoughts except for the electric hum of the computer and fax machine. There was no sound of television or the washer and dryer coming from the other rooms in the house either, and certainly no sound upstairs. Stephen knew Marie had gone to bed, even though she did not come to tell him good night. Tonight he would stay up late, but not to prepare an affidavit or review a legal agreement between business partners. He was preoccupied with making sense out of another contractual arrangement in his life; specifically, where his parental obligations to his adult children stood. He prided himself for his loyalty and took seriously his commitments to raise his children until legal age, providing the best education and upbringing he and Marie could offer to ensure their children's future success. He truly believed he loved his family but could not help but compartmentalize his feelings when he needed to step back and reconsider what he deemed best for his family. Whenever a client was sued or faced some other conflict with a neighbour where a fence was built, he would help provide practical reassurance by clarifying the precise terms of the client's legal obligations and rights. He often told clients that conflict was not something to fear but rather an opportunity to strengthen their resolve, bringing the full force of the law to deflect unfounded allegations, or to mitigate risk with entrepreneurial pursuits. He was good at what he did and clients paid gratefully for his expertise. His successful legal practice continually reinforced the wisdom of defining boundaries and operating confidently within those terms.

This stance served Marie well in their own marital relationship. When she felt he intruded on her space, whether it was the privacy she demanded when getting dressed and doing her makeup, or having separate bank accounts, or making decisions together regarding where they would invest or go on holidays, she could easily remind him of their previously agreed upon terms. She too would respect his claims when she was rightly accused of interfering in his rights, especially when he reminded her of the demanding hours required as a partner in his law firm, which the entire family benefitted from financially. She accepted those many evenings he spent in the den, and always knocked on the French doors before entering, even when she brought him a tea. Their volunteer work was an experiment in trying to share roles as equals on the parish social justice committee in which they could cast separate votes, and voice different opinions, as evident in the decision earlier today at the retreat. They both had to respect their separate committee positions, and it was inappropriate to let their own marital relationship interfere with their fiduciary responsibilities.

It had to be clean, especially given the perceived conflict of interest having a couple serving simultaneously on the committee that the parish was willing to experiment in an effort to engage more couple ministry.

Even when it came to parenting Rebecca and Michael when they were young, it was relatively easy with the boundary-setting discipline Stephen consistently modeled. As the primary wage earner and being absent so often from home, he never interfered in Marie's parental decisions, especially when the kids tried to circumvent their authority. The parents had discussed and agreed the rational thing to do was to ensure one approach, and even if he disagreed with her in private, Stephen would always back her up in front of the kids. This was effective parental strategy for years, convincing both Marie and Stephen that it gave their children the secure foundation for them to thrive.

But with adolescence, the rule setting with the children became more blurred. The agreed-upon framework needed to be nuanced, which Marie instinctively understood, especially when their young teen daughter privately confided in her mother, insisting she not tell Stephen about her first period, for example. Neither did Rebecca want her mother to say anything about relationship conflicts she had with other girls at school, nor the accompanying insecurities around her body image and recurring acne. What was once a clear arrangement between parents regarding the need for consensus concerning major interventions slowly relegated Stephen to an on-a-need-to-know basis, at least as regards Rebecca. In part because of Stephen's own awkwardness in relating to a young teen girl's experiences, coupled by Rebecca's relative uneventful transition through adolescent, Stephen was able to accept this flexing of their parental contractual arrangements. He even believed he was growing more used to ambiguity and not being in the know, trusting Marie's judgment as long as she was "talking to Rebecca."

However, Michael's entry into adolescence changed all this, for exactly the opposite reasons. To Stephen, Michael was troubled, and he was male. Or at least that is what he expected him to be, despite the challenges of competing with another male presence in the house, even one who openly declared himself as gay. While it was easy to accept the contractual terms he and Marie shared regarding Rebecca, with Michael he had no precedent, no case law, no ability to control this area of his life. And it scared the hell out of Stephen. His own feelings of inadequacy led Stephen to be more controlling. And though he would never admit it, it also led to more self-doubt and uncertainty. Only when alone in a dimly lit study could he risk acknowledging this to himself.

The kids had since moved out and he was increasingly finding himself alone. Stephen's parish committee work with Marie served more as a convenient distraction, providing some pretense to avoid the implications of what living parallel lives forced them to accept. As long as Stephen could portray the public face of their couple ministry to others, he still had this one false claim to hang onto. But after this afternoon's conversation with Marie on the drive home from St. Benedict's, even Stephen began to wonder. It threatened him that Marie may have given up the illusion. Without her doing her part, he was forced to look within.

He looked for a fragment of memory that was kept neatly filed in a book somewhere in the den. A fact he once deemed irrelevant, which he might have put aside several years ago. As a lawyer, his book shelves contained many such facts that helped him research a current legal problem if he knew where to look. It was another way that he could draw neat firm boundaries around his life, knowing at any given time he could consider a new perspective if required, and on his terms. When he could close the door, as he did tonight, separating the den from the rest of his house without worry of exposing his own vulnerability. But given the glass panel French doors, he doubted he would have been able to do so if Marie was still up.

On a middle shelf near the desk and next to the family photo albums, he pulled off Michael and Rebecca's high school yearbooks. Neither of their kids took their yearbooks when they moved out. Rebecca said she didn't have the room when she went to live in university residence. Besides, she always liked the idea of some of her childhood memorabilia staying behind in the family home. She knew it would be safe and untouched, allowing her to pull it out if she was particularly nostalgic during a visit home. Like her father, she could always reach for the memories whenever she needed to do so; except for Rebecca, they were always relevant and meaningful. Rebecca saw her yearbooks as a way of keeping her connected to her past, but for Stephen, they were a means of keeping particular memories at bay, to be kept out of sight on a shelf.

Michael was different when it came to such things. Stephen wondered if he cared at all about photo albums and yearbooks, or even remembered they existed. Whereas Stephen feared repeating the mistake of Lot's wife by looking back and bringing judgment upon the house, it was as if his son was bound by another divine command. Michael was never tempted to look back; neither from a place of guilt nor curiosity. Once Michael tasted freedom when he moved out of the home, and more emphatically, told his parents he would never come back, it would be difficult to take back his words. He would never again allow his spirit to be incarcerated by a father's disapproving look. It was such looks that could turn even the most spirited ambitions into a pillar of salt.

Only Rebecca savoured traditions. Like her father, she needed quiet times in the den, sitting in the rich burgundy leather chair, which itself represented tradition and history to look through old pictures. She could see the high school memories marked a dividing line from the family they once knew, from what they had become in recent years. Both father and daughter sought to bridge the different chapters of their lives. Rebecca reminisced to try to understand what happened to their family and what was still redeemable. Whereas Stephen looked back in order to assign blame, finding clues as to when Michael's behaviour drove a wedge between father and son, and, as evident by the argument earlier in the day on the way home, between his parents. Much as he often did in his study in preparing for a legal case, he searched for evidence to justify his defense in asking Michael to leave; a decision he increasingly found himself defending alone. He could not afford to reveal any weakness in his decision, even if Marie wavered. He did not yield at the retreat today despite the pressure to acquiesce, and he would not yield on this, either. To do this he had to be strong.

He flipped through the pages of his son's and daughter's high school yearbooks, pausing occasionally to study certain photos of his children's friends and teachers. Even the most disciplined mind could not inadvertently begin to wander through the memories and become lost in nostalgia. But this evening, Stephen was looking for something specific and would not lose his focus. Besides, it was not just photos in which he searched, but some scribbled words he recalled a classmate wrote in either his son's yearbook or his daughter's that aroused his curiosity. A comment that he read once that bothered him, but dismissed at the time as merely a high school graduate's histrionics on the way to a long night of partying.

He looked first in Michael's yearbook, which had only a few postscript testaments by friends. That wasn't a surprise, as he never knew what his son or his friends were thinking about back then anyways, other than the crude drawings of penises and other sexual innuendo that provided some insight. Still, he went through the exercise of checking, telling himself unconvincingly that he may have previously overlooked some clue within its pages that would help him understand who his son was, and what he had become. However, he surmised what he was looking for was in Rebecca's book anyways, and all he was really doing was delaying facing the truth. For it was not a question of what his son had become; rather, it was what Stephen had become that was far more painful.

He closed the yearbook and tossed it on the desk, pausing before picking up Rebecca's. They looked the same with the matching school crest on the white cover with blue lettering, distinguishable only by the graduation dates. Rebecca's *Class of 1984* memoir depicted a younger looking Grade 10 photograph of her brother. Even in this picture, Stephen could see his son was beginning to take on a new identity with the wild looking haircut—if it could be called a hair style at all. He remembered the fight about that incident when Michael refused to cut his hair for picture day in the fall. To the casual observer, the boy looked no different than the other exaggerated expressions among a typical high school class of teens, but for Stephen it was yet another reminder of his eroding power as a father that was obvious to him now. If Michael looked at his Grade 10 photograph, would he recognize the power he wrestled from his father? By the time of his 1986 graduation, his class picture took on an even more self-assured look of confidence.

It was reassuring to Stephen to see his daughter as he still knew her. Younger, yes, but reflecting in her eyes was a treasured place where a father's love and influence endured. She was not fighting the world and her father as was her brother. It was also comforting to Stephen to see many scribbled notes of gratitude and well wishes from her class mates as they reminisced on their journey together in high school, eagerly anticipating crossing over a threshold into adulthood. It was evident Rebecca and her friends shared many achievements and memories, and she had a positive role model on others throughout her teen years. He wanted to keep this image of her as strong and confident alive always, knowing she embraced the values that he tried to instill in both his children. Such pictures of Rebecca pleased Stephen, reassuring him that she would be okay in life. It was vindication that he was a good father, despite his son's rejection.

Of course, Rebecca had her own share of friends' veiled comments interspersed in her yearbook about partying and other risky behaviour that suggested not everything Stephen taught her was taken to heart. But it was somehow easier to overlook those transgressions in his daughter than the graffiti images in Michael's.

Stephen spent more time looking than expected. He was beginning to doubt if what he was looking for was in her yearbook after all. Finally he turned the page towards the back cover and saw, written in large flowing strokes in faded black ink:

Better luck in the future Becca. Here's to all the beer spilt and tears shed. Don't let him hold you back. The sooner you move out, move away, and move on… the better. Luv ya forever! Cindy H.

He read the passage several times to be certain this was the same note he recalled seeing not long after her grad party seven years ago. At the time, he thought Cindy H was talking about Rebecca's brother. It didn't dawn on him that it could be anyone else. Rebecca worked hard in school and busted her ass while Michael goofed off, which was the cause of many family arguments, especially when Rebecca complained about the expectations placed on her. Naturally then, Stephen surmised, Rebecca would have vented about the tension at home with her friends, blaming her brother for being so difficult. She would have become emotional when drinking at some high school party with Cindy H, saying it wasn't fair that she was ignored while her jerk brother got all the attention. Stephen imagined this evening as he always did how difficult this would have been for Rebecca, and even more so if her mother and father didn't give her enough credit for what she had to put up with. The note was simply an expression of solidarity between two high school girls; Cindy H encouraging his daughter not to be held back or defined by her brother's irresponsible behaviour. If Stephen had failed to notice his daughter's struggle in high school in her relationship to Michael, he vowed he wouldn't fail her again by letting her brother's issues overshadow her.

Still, Stephen could not completely convince himself of this interpretation of Cindy H's note as did previously. Marie's words earlier today still stung, and he could not push away the doubts. "Was Rebecca's friend referring to Michael, or to me?" Cindy H's note could easily substitute his name for Michael's and still make sense. As a lawyer, he could not deny this possibility. "If it was true, and the sooner Rebecca left home to get away from *me,* then why didn't she tell me? What could I have done to push her away?"

Stephen suddenly felt very alone in the study. Marie was not there to reassure him that there was nothing to worry about, allaying fears that his entire relationship with his daughter could be called into question, that it was irrational to think that way. Rebecca was not there to talk with him, either, laughing as she would at her father's private joke, knowing they shared the same sense of wry humour. He always felt so close to her when they joked around but now he wondered if there was a part of her that was laughing at him all these years. "If I had been so wrong about her before, could I still be wrong? What else may be going on in her life that I have no clue about? Does Marie know at least?" He resolved to talk with Rebecca when she was over next, or better, he would call her.

He read the yearbook note several more times, trying to reassure himself that it was irrational and he was reading more into it because he was tired. In law, he knew that all plausible explanations should be considered, but he also knew by the principle known as Ockham's Razor that the simpler and reasonable interpretation was probably likely. He had spent an entire career arguing the facts of cases based on logic and reasonability, distinguishing credible evidence from speculation, but tonight he wondered if his ability to interpret the facts as presented before him in Cindy H's note was in doubt.

But he could not accept this was the case. He *was* close to his daughter. How could he doubt that? He always meant well. Even her brother knew Dad was close to her, despite Michael's own estrangement from the family. And while Stephen was prepared tonight to ask if his decision to kick Michael out was right, only if merely a concession to Marie, he was not prepared to accept he had been wrong about both his children. To consider he had been in entrenched denial for so many years was unacceptable. To believe this would be to accept he had been wrong about everything he knew of parenthood, and the sometimes tough decisions that had to be made for the family. In fact, even today at the retreat, arguments were put forward regarding accepting some actions to prevent a greater harm from occurring. "Was I not also giving Michael a chance to grow up and learn an invaluable lesson, even though it is hard?" Throwing an adult child out of the house would never be easy, Stephen believed, but sometimes it was necessary.

No, he had to stay the course, even if it caused strain in his marriage. Cindy H may never know this, yet he had plans for Marie and the kids. He put the yearbooks back onto the shelf, pushing them neatly and evenly back into place, as neatly and evenly as he pushed the memories of regret far back in his mind.

Stephen got up and walked over to the pedestal globe in the office he once received as a gift from a client. He ran his fingers thoughtfully over the texture ridges of the globe representing the Earth's irregular terrain. He knew nothing was ever smooth in life or without blemish and yet, despite impassable mountain terrain and vast bodies of water separating the continents, they were all part of one interdependent world. His family was also marred by division and conflict, but he knew it was his responsibility to not give into anything that could further divide the family. Allowing Michael to come home would only condone his behaviour, which Stephen would in turn resent, resulting in more emotional stress and even risk of physical altercation. Reversing the decision would be scandalous to his sister, who sacrificed so much to get her university education and a job in her chosen field. It would also undermine his parental authority in setting the rules for the house. It would justify irresponsible behaviour that Stephen judged to be immoral, compromising his own conscience if he did so.

There was an axis that ran through the globe, and in like fashion, the values and principles around which he expected the family to revolve must be respected. He also held this to be true in law, building a successful practice and reputation as a professional who consistently interpreted what justice demanded. The same career, he pointed out, that his wife and children benefitted from financially. He was a good provider and made sacrifices along the way for his family, which they were called to reciprocate.

The more Stephen mused, the more justified he felt, despite the vocal opposition he endured both at home and in the parish today. He needed to be strong and resolved, even if he was judged unfairly by his own family. He trusted in time his wife and children would see the wisdom of his approach and come around. "How could they call me arrogant if in my heart I am doing what I truly believe is best for all, especially given the cost of my convictions?" He felt certain that his children needed him as much as they needed their mother. And at the parish, his vision was no less important and compelling than what a young inexperienced parish priest could ever imagine.

The thought of Fr. Bao brought back a conversation he had with Marie following an education session they attended at the parish several years ago, before Fr. Bao arrived. It was about the Rule of St. Benedict in everyday life, in honour of their parish patron saint. Marie pointed out afterwards a specific statement in the Rule that she thought equally applied to parenthood:

"Stephen, I want you to see this." She read from the reflection document they brought home.

"It's from chapter sixty-four in the Rule. Listen to this: 'He must hate faults but love the brothers. When he must punish them, he should use prudence and avoid extremes; otherwise, by rubbing too hard to remove the rust, he may break the vessel.'"

Marie looked up expectedly. "What do you think of that?"

"St. Benedict didn't have to raise teenagers."

"You know what he's getting at, Stephen. You don't want to break their spirits."

"I have never hit the kids, Marie, and you know that."

"I'm not talking about physically hurting them, but you ride them sometimes."

"I get after Michael, but do you blame me? I found a pot plant in his room the other day."

"You also get after Rebecca."

"No, I don't. She's a good kid."

"So is Michael. They both need you. Not for you to chastise them but to give them your confidence."

"I'm always praising Rebecca. Look how great she's doing in school."

"But you are pressuring her, as if she has to be perfect to make up for Michael. Like you have already written off Michael and withdrawn your support, but Rebecca has to be even better to make up for that. She just wants to be a normal teenager."

"I suppose she told you this," said Stephen defensively.

"She is telling you this all the time, if only you would listen to her."

Stephen felt the pain of this exchange in the study tonight. Words he obviously chose to forget. Michael kept pushing his buttons and he had to admit to his shame that he stopped seeing Rebecca for who she was, but rather only what she represented. In some respects, he saw Michael more clearly than he did his daughter, despite the conflict that defined the relationship between father and son. Even now, he still saw Rebecca for her accomplishments, what she did for a living, and the money she earned, but he related to Michael just for who he was, despite the disappointment and sense of burden he felt towards his son. "How could I be so wrong?" thought Stephen.

He reverently spun the globe with his finger as he turned to look outside the front window of the study. The sky was dark and overcast, as it was often in Vancouver. Funny, he thought, that when Michael and Rebecca were young he tried to take advantage of those rare clear warm summer nights to bring out the small telescope they owned to the backyard to look at the moon, or to try find the rings of Saturn or Jupiter's moons. He taught them that even when the sky was enveloped in cloud, or awash in the brilliant light of day, the stars and moon had not gone away. The objects in the sky were always there, and it was just a matter of waiting for the right conditions to bring them back into view. Just as their house had not disappeared when they walked among the trees in the ravine below their house, or if conflict got in the way of their relationship with each other, they still had each other. They had to believe that even if their vision was hindered, they should not give up. He warned them often that people would come into their lives who might try to obstruct their vision and it was up to them to stand up for themselves and not give in to pressure.

Stephen did not have an answer for how such parental advice applied to him given the inconsistent example he set. He obviously did not know a lot about his children. He never understood how Michael could be led by such a different set of values than what Marie and he taught them, especially compared to Rebecca.

He sat down at his desk and pulled out a pad of paper. Reaching for a pen, he wrote today's date at the top and paused, searching for words to begin the letter to his son. The light from his favourite green lamp on his desk encouraged him. He knew it should start with 'Dear Michael', but what should come next? What was it that he wanted to say? "That I'm sorry?" thought Stephen. "That I was wrong?" "That I wish we could begin again and I want you to come back?"

He tried different words in his mind, imagining his son's reaction upon reading the letter. He wondered if his son would put the letter down and sob or rip it up in anger. "Probably just forget to open it, given where his head is at most days," concluded Stephen in disgust. The momentarily compulsion to reach out to his son to ask for forgiveness and to give a father's blessing passed as old feelings of resentment and hurt returned. Though he was tempted to chase after Michael, he knew it was for his son's good to find his own way. He had previously figured his son would grow out of the partying and eccentric behaviour, but this evening he was reminded what he harboured in his heart: that his son was indeed lost from view. Michael had been adrift in a fog of his own making and it was only up to him to find his way back. It would do Michael no good to rescue him. Stephen's own astronomy lessons were apparently lost on him.

Instead, Stephen said a silent prayer for his son before picking up a law journal to read until he got sleepy enough to go to bed.

CHAPTER 19

Mai Ly was dressing when Luc banged on the door of the decrepit hotel room she shared with the other women, hollering to let him in. She opened the door and Luc pushed past her, filling the room with his big frame and even bigger voice.

"Why the fuck aren't you outside?"

"I'm almost ready, Luc. I was working this afternoon and I just had a nap. Give me a break."

"That's not what I heard. The girls said you were talking to the cops. Give me a good reason I don't fucking break your arm?" Luc said menacingly as he grabbed hold of her.

"Ow, that's hurts, Luc. You're going to bruise me," Mai Ly protested.

"Yeah, we don't want to bruise the goods," he replied cynically, throwing her arm back.

He glared at her, as if he was looking through her, testing her.

"What did the cops want?"

"They wanted to know about Magda. She's dead."

"Yeah, I heard the little cunt was dead, her and her baby. No wonder she was no good working. Who would want to fuck her with a gut sticking out? She should have taken care of that problem earlier."

"Aren't you a gentleman," Mai Ly retorted.

"What I am is your man, and the man needs to be paid. Where's her money?"

"I don't know. With the rest of it."

Luc went to the fridge and opened the little freezer door, which was empty save for a can of Folgers coffee with a plastic lid. He grabbed at it and pulled off the lid.

"What the fuck?" he snarled, looking into the nearly empty can containing only a few twenty dollar bills. His face turned bright red. "Where's all my money, bitch? There should be thousands in there! From you as well."

"I just have some from last night. I didn't have time to put it in." She reached for the money from her push up bra and threw it on the table.

"What about the rest of it? I'm gone for one night to have me some good time with real women and you bitches can't even do your fucking job."

Mai Ly cowered as fear overwhelmed her. Luc grabbed the money from the table and slapped her with the back of his other hand.

"Where's my money?"

"It's all I have, I promise!" Mai Ly cried, covering her head for what she knew would come next. He pulled out his belt and hit her repeatedly as she crumpled to the floor despite desperate pleas for him to stop.

"Do I not deserve a night off? Can't the man have a little holiday? Where the fuck is your sense of responsibility?" he yelled in between blows. She sobbed convulsively on the floor, shaking, her cheap mascara streaking her face.

"Pull yourself together and get out on the street or I will come back to give you more, you hear?"

He slammed the door behind him as she tried to get herself upright before falling back, as the welts glistened red and hot.

★ ★ ★

Fr. Bao drove down East Hastings Street slowly, looking for Mai Ly on the stretch she now frequented. He had already pulled off his priest collar and wore a cap. He had seen others before when talking with Mai Ly on Gore that he recognized from the East Van neighbourhood, and even once thought he saw a parishioner in a car pulled over at the street corner. The last thing he wanted now was to be spotted circling the strip on a Saturday night. It had started to rain and it was hard to see clearly through the car window as he drove slowly. He rolled down his passenger window part way to see the faces of the endless sea of addicts, dealers, prostitutes and other lost souls looking for that fix that would bring temporary relief of the pain in their broken lives. He turned right on Cordova and made another loop back on Hastings, and then again another few times. To those on the street, his cover under darkness and rain was long blown. He was just another john looking for his own pain relief.

Mai Ly scored a dime bag of crack with money she had kept for herself, often using her anus to conceal a meager portion of the earnings. Fr. Bao finally saw her, staggering down the sidewalk in a drug-induced high, aggravated by her recent beating. He pulled alongside as she walked and called out repeatedly until she looked over. Squinting, she peered into the car, smiling absently before waving Fr. Bao off. She continued her Eastside Shuffle up the street.

Fr. Bao stopped the car and jumped out, continuing to call out after her.

"Mai! Mai Ly! Wait up."

He got in front of her, putting both hands on her shoulder in an attempt to brace her as she stumbled. He gasped seeing the bruises on her face up close. Her right eye was nearly swollen shut.

"Oh, my God! What happened to you?"

"Nothing. Nothing. Lemme go."

"Let me take you out of here, Mai. You should go to the hospital."

"I gotta go to work. Let me go." She brushed past him and Fr. Bao reached out for her arm, the same one Luc had viciously grabbed earlier.

"Ow! Let me go!"

"No, Mai. You don't have to live like this. Let me take care of you. Come back with me. We can go right now. C'mon, Mai Ly. Come home with me."

"I don't want to. Get out of my way."

"Stop, Mai. You are more than this. I can save you."

147

"You can't save me. You can't save anyone. Go home. You don't belong here."

"You belong with me, Mai Ly. I can take you home with me. I know some people who can help, get you into programs, make sure you're safe," he pleaded.

"Like you helped Magda? I heard she went to you and look what happened. Get lost."

Fr. Bao put both his arms on her shoulders again, but immediately she pushed them off. He grabbed on again, clinging to her, clinging to his past, to fading hope.

"I said lemme go!"

She swung wildly at Fr. Bao, stumbling before falling to the ground. He reached down to lift her up. Instinctively Mai Ly bit him on the hand. She screamed and other Eastside Shufflers stopped to see the commotion. A few people moved towards them.

"Get lost you jerk! I don't wanna see you ever again, Priest. You hear me, Priest? Get loss and never come back!"

"Hey, buddy, you heard the lady. Let her go," said one.

"Hey, honey, I'll do you if she won't. I never did a priest before," said another.

Holding his hand and winching in pain, Fr. Bao looked at the man who confronted him, and the other prostitutes and two-time hustlers gathering around them. Even then, he was still ready to fight for her, but the look on Mai Ly's face told him it was over. Her eyes were full of contempt. She didn't just reject him, but the life he imagined for her, a life he could never fill let alone the one he once held out for A'nh. His failure to rescue Mai Ly brought him back again to the beach, unable to prevent his sister and mother from being carried off. Once again, on the streets of Vancouver's Downtown Eastside, he was alone.

Dejectedly, he returned to his car and drove home.

CHAPTER 20

In a world so vast, two individuals share their grief.
All is part of them, especially their eyes.
He becomes her; and she, him.

The international boarding area was busy this August evening in 1993, busier that Bao would have thought. It had been years since he had flown overseas. He was nine when he finally arrived in Canada, alone after a long flight from Singapore. Even though he didn't really understand it at the time, he could see that the immigration process was exceedingly complicated and time-consuming. Now, just fourteen years later, it felt so surreal given how simple it was to book a flight with a travel agent, pick up his ticket, and show up at the airport.

He flew earlier in the afternoon from Winnipeg. As the sky darkened outside the airport terminal building in Vancouver, the glass panes from which he sat opposite in the boarding area slowly began to reflect back light as his own thoughts transitioned further inward. He sought out a quiet spot as far away as possible from the throng of other passengers milling about at their respective gates, anxiously waiting to board flights that would take them to destinations across Asia, like Hong Kong, where Bao would be flying this evening before connecting elsewhere. Maybe even Vietnam, Boa imagined. He knew others from his local Vietnamese community had gone back since diplomatic relations were reestablished, and with relatively straight forward arrangements organized by his travel agent in Winnipeg, he too could have gone home.

Home? The word sounded so strange, thought Bao. Where was home now? He moved from Somerset four years ago to attend the University of Manitoba, staying in residence at the campus near the south end of Winnipeg as his adoptive parents were still working and unable to relocate to the city at that time. During Bao's undergraduate program, he faithfully went home most weekends unless winter road conditions made it unsafe to drive on the rural highways to Somerset. Michelle cried when he left for university the first time, and each departure after Sunday dinner was an emotional experience for her, despite how much she tried to disguise her feelings.

Bao was her only son, which was a miracle in itself given how long she and her husband waited to adopt a child until the Boat People exodus provided an opportunity. Even then, adoption was wrought with immigration delays and uncertainties, and prospective parents were never sure of the outcome until the child actually arrived and was placed in their care. When Michelle and André received word from authorities, it still took time before Bao was home with them. That was the hardest part of the wait, when expectations were raised and parents started to imagine life with their child. Michelle had begun to love Bao long before he arrived, and so it was understandable that his leaving home was a process that would take time to work through, one weekend at a time.

Bao called her Mom, and always acknowledged her publicly as his mother, but his skin colour and facial features mercifully excused both of them from having to explain to people each time that she was not his *real* mother. They could both express their affection without feeling guilty in being perceived by others as insensitive and thoughtless, relegating the one who actually bore him to the sidelines as but a mere footnote in his life story. Bao's Vietnamese mother lived on in the unspoken space between Bao and Michelle, requiring no explanation to justify. Her presence was simply accepted. And while Bao never knew his real dad, he grew to calling his adoptive father by his first name, not out of disrespect to André; on the contrary, more because of the friendship they shared. André always praised his son and gave him the security to know he was loved and belonged, even though another home claimed part of Bao's heart.

As twilight turned the terminal glass opaque he saw the mirror image of his life coming into view, which in recent months had increasingly tormented him. However, it was not the empty space of a mother or father lost that interrupted his sleep, but that of his sister, An'h.

In the corner of their eyes, a teardrop appears,
Emerging from their deep, silent pain.
It glistens for a moment then moves down the cheek, leaving a wet trail behind.

Perhaps it was memories of his mother and sister that hollowed out space in his heart, deepening his spirit of compassion for others that changed him. Or the example and influence of the Carmelite Sisters who cared for him at the internment camps. Or perhaps his upbringing by Michelle and André in Somerset, who taught him about unconditional love. For whatever reason, sometime during the end of the second year of university, the influence of all these people and his reflection on his inner experience led him to discern a call to the priesthood. At first, he kept these thoughts to himself and spoke only with a priest mentor at St. Paul's College at the University of Manitoba, who offered him impartial guidance and support. When he finally did tell his adoptive parents, Bao knew it reawakened the emptiness they still carried, especially for Michelle. Not only the emptiness in not having children of their own, but also by implication of his announcement of a call to the celibate priesthood, in not having grandchildren, either. They had already given up the idea of someone carrying on the family name, since they always wanted to honour Bao's roots, giving their young son the choice to reclaim his own surname when he came of age. Understandably, Bao's announcement was just another painful reminder of what Michelle missed out on in life.

As always, Bao felt André's supportive love and knew his adopted father spent time alone with Michelle to reassure her of what she had and always would through the gift of their son. It took a while, but Bao noticed Michelle was becoming more visibly relaxed with each subsequent weekend that he came home to visit. She began to trust that he would never forget them if they gave him their blessing and let him go. In fact, the idea of their son's budding vocation grew on Michelle, from shocked revelation to eventually a place of curiosity in trying to understand what this would mean for their family. In time, she mustered the courage to ask where he would study after his arts degree, hoping it wouldn't be too far away. Then the question was where he might be sent to minister afterwards. "Could you ever be assigned to the parish in Somerset?" she would ask. Rather than dreading the loss of her son, Michelle secretly saw this as an opportunity to proudly boast and celebrate his leadership role in the community. She knew this was probably unlikely, but had to hold onto this remote possibility for fear of confronting the reality of his impending leave taking all at once. Despite her brave front, Bao knew she held back a bit, careful not to expose her pain in mourning the loss of not having a baby of her own that she always felt unfairly sentenced.

It was hard then for Bao to announce before he graduated with his arts degree just a few months ago the plans that brought him to the international boarding area this evening. He told his parents that before going to Newman Seminary in Edmonton, he first needed to travel overseas, to search for his real mother and sister. Leaving the province and going away for seminary was already hard enough for Michelle, so he had to break this news slowly, allowing her to digest it one piece at a time. Bao started by explaining that he was going to take a vacation, and then maybe work a year first before seminary. The momentary relief Michelle felt was dashed as his entire plan was laid out and all the old feelings came crashing upon her.

She thought this was settled five years ago. At that time, their naïve seventeen year-old son pleaded to his adopted parents to send him to Thailand to search for his lost family. As the finality of his last year of high school dawned, it resurfaced the intense feelings of his own losses, forcing to bring closure to another chapter of his life without his mother and sister. Through many emotional and tearful discussions at the beginning of grade twelve, Michelle and André were able to talk reason with their idealistic son, reminding him of the countless phone calls and letters they made together over the years with immigration authorities, all to no avail. That was a dark time in Michelle's life as she feared he would just quit school and leave, walking out of their lives for good. Bao could only imagine what André said during those uncertain months in the fall of 1988. Still, they were careful not to rob their son of hope, assuring themselves that he would come to some place of acceptance.

But now it was different. Over the past several years he had become a man. Their gift to him for university graduation was the open ticket he carried now in his tote bag, next to the silk scarf with his sister's initials. Michelle's tears at the Winnipeg airport before he boarded his plane to Vancouver only served to strengthen his resolve to leave. There could be no response and sustained call to life in the priesthood if he could not be faithful to what summoned forth from his own history, to at least try. He looked back to wave at his parents once clearing security, seeing written on Michelle's face the same look of anguish he imagined his birth mother would have always been haunted by as the boat was pushed out to sea.

Bao caught the flinch of his hand in the darkened terminal glass as he sipped from the tea he bought. He remembered after waving at his parents earlier today that he looked down and away, knowing André's arm would be on Michelle, reassuring her yet again that it was going to be okay.

But the dream begins to slow itself, and they separate.

He sees reflected in the tear his own face.

He longs to reach out to her, but he can't.

He sat back in the airport terminal seat, looking beyond his reflection in the glass to the pulsating lights surrounding the fuselage and wings of planes taxiing on the dark, wet tarmac below. These lights, including the plane's invisible identification signature beam, helped controllers track the multitude of flights that crossed back and forth over the Pacific Ocean that night. So much traffic, Bao thought, and yet few planes ever lost. Yes, they would occasionally crash upon takeoff or landing, but there was always a black box that would confirm the plane's identity and recordings to piece together what transpired before the accident. It might take months to fully understand but there would be closure for grieving families, and lessons learned for the airlines to help prevent similar tragedies in the future. But with only his sister's scarf and a worn photograph of her he carried in his pocket, how fleeting these two locating lights were to help guide his path towards possible closure. There was nothing but rumours he recalled from the internment camps years ago providing some faint clues, leads that might require confronting dangerous people and risking his own life. Bao felt suspended between one mother pulling him forward in his search and another pleading him never to leave.

More people started to gather in the seats around him, and the boarding gate staff arrived shortly afterward to prepare for the next flight. His reprieve from the din in the airport was over, but it was a welcome distraction from the guilt he felt. He needed to look ahead towards the horizon that would soon greet the darkness of this night. He thought that Michelle and André would have since arrived home in Somerset after dropping him off at the airport and then stocking up on groceries in Winnipeg. They would have found the letter he wrote them and left on the dining room table to say goodbye, thanking them for their continued support and prayers. He tried to explain again in writing why he had to go, reassuring them he would be safe and would keep in touch. Bao wondered if it would have been better to have not left anything. It was already hard for them to think they would not see him much once he eventually left for seminary in Edmonton, even though they were busy with their own volunteer work at the local parish. But at the same time, he did not want them to think he was walking out on their lives forever. They needed to hold onto something too.

The truth was, thought Bao; it was becoming harder to come back to *that* home. Again he wondered, where was his real home? One leg was straddled in the home of his past and the other in his present, but he felt rooted in neither. It was necessary to leave to find where he really belonged, and to whom. He wondered if he could ever adequately explain this to his well-meaning and loving parents who had sacrificed so much to raise him, reassuring them that he wasn't giving up their family. Living in residence the past four years gave Bao the space necessary to think clearly. In high school, he still lacked the insight to articulate a cogent plan. At seventeen he only had the words of a poem he wrote to express his sense of longing, which he left unsigned on his English literature teacher's desk over lunchtime, never claiming identity when she asked the class to whom the poem belonged. He wanted someone to know how he felt, even if expressed anonymously. He had no rational argument to successfully lobby his parents' support to send him overseas, just the expressed longings captured with a few scribbled lines.

André offered to take him overseas if he wanted after he finished high school. As grade twelve graduation neared, however, Bao pretended he was preoccupied with getting ready for university and moving into residence, leaving André to believe it was just a phase that had thankfully passed. But Michelle sensed otherwise and dreaded this day. The note she would read later on the dining room table and cry over only confirmed what she had known would eventually come. She had no choice but to let him go and pray for his safe return.

He cries out, "Wait, wait little girl,
for one day I will wipe away your tears."

Bao got up to check the electronic terminal board for an update on his departure time and gate number. He tossed what was left of his cold tea in a trash can and went for a walk in the airport to stretch his legs before boarding his long overnight flight to Hong Kong. In twenty-four hours, he thought expectantly, he would be in Bangkok, where his sister was awaiting his return. Waiting all these years for her brother to free her. He was alone now but smiled to himself, thinking of flying back with A'nh to begin their new life and home together.

CHAPTER 21

The phone call came as no surprise. Tanis imagined many times how she would react if the care centre called to say her dad took a turn for the worse, or died in his sleep. Each day was becoming harder for her to visit, seeing the person before her slowly, almost imperceptibly deteriorating. A mere shadow of the father she knew and loved. Loved? Tanis wondered if the love for her dad left a long time ago with his memories.

All she could muster was some sense of family obligation, maybe at best, benign affection. But love?

"When did that feeling leave me?" she asked herself. It had been a long time since she had cried for her dad or felt filled with any semblance of joy for the father who always stood by her. The person who never failed to tell his only daughter how proud he was of her. She was once his little girl. Now, it was like she was a stranger to him; and he to her.

She listened calmly as the nurse explained that her dad suffered an apparent stroke early this morning and was now paralyzed on his left side, with laboured breathing and progressive mottling of his extremities. She told Tanis that she should come right away, clarifying to come to his room as they would not be transferring her dad to hospital.

She hung up the phone purposely and sat on the side of her bed for a moment, absorbing the news, thinking what she would have to do next. There was no need to rush, she decided, feeling no closer or further from her dad in the privacy of her condo than actually being with him at the centre. But she did not want to avoid going there, either. She took a shower, dressed and gathered a few numbers she thought she would need to let her cousins know, as well to make funeral arrangements. Maybe even call in someone for prayers.

And Sandy. She wanted to let him know she would be gone for a few days if and when her dad died. She decided to wait until she got to the care centre and talked with the doctor before calling him, just in case.

She did, however, phone for a cab. Even though it was a short walk from her place, she did not feel like being exposed for all to view on the street. The cab driver asked no questions and mercifully spared Tanis any small talk. She simply paid him his fare and walked in. Today there was no sunlight peering through the atrium glass, just the usual Vancouver dreariness, absent precipitation. Neither rain nor any tears fell this Sunday morning.

Tanis held her dad's hand, trying to remember the warmth of his touch when he came for visits and hugged her, and especially when he brushed her cheek tenderly in saying goodbye, as was his custom. She had a cognitive memory of their lives shared, but could not feel what it was like anymore. It seemed as if her dad died long ago, and this was all a part of an extended goodbye. The physician on call had explained that her dad had a massive stroke and was not expected to live long. He diligently informed her that they would provide comfort measures only, so as not to prolong his dying nor burden him with treatments or tests that would not alter the outcome. She agreed, but in the secret of her heart, she wished they could just give him something to end it all now.

She tried praying, asking God to take him. The words she voiced silently as she sat next to his bed seemed so disingenuous, as though already half expecting God would disappoint her, leaving both of them to suffer, to make the goodbye longer and more painful. The chaplain came by and attempted to engage her, and although he was sensitive and respectful, she wished only to be alone to keep vigil, waiting for the end that she had been waiting to come. The end that would finally conclude the cruel indictment she felt had been levied against them.

She answered her pager; relieved she could step away from her father's room out of a competing sense of duty. Tanis was told by the forensic officer that DNA tests confirmed that Magda was the mother of the baby, as the other circumstantial evidence pointed. She also learned that Baby Jane Doe was going to be discharged from the BC Children's and Women's Hospital early next week under the auspices of a court appointed guardian until such time they could determine next of kin and try to unite the baby, if not with the father, then at least with other related family. With all the news in the media, especially the weekend reports Nargis Lehkar had been running on the radio, the public had been calling the hospital and leaving messages with child and family services to inquire about adopting the baby girl. She wondered who would care to claim the mother's body that remained in the morgue at St. Paul's Hospital. That story didn't seem to be as newsworthy, it seemed.

She was also told that the social services unit had followed up on some leads Mai Ly provided of other women who likely had contact with Magda, learning further details about her family in Poland, but there was still so much they did not know about her. Other than Mai Ly, who kept her recent conversation with Magda in confidence, no one knew when she came or how she ended up on the street. People speculated she had a sordid past. What else would drive an attractive young woman to a life that was so degrading and violent if not a victim of degradation and violence herself?

Those who looked after Tanis' father in recent weeks may have equally wondered about his past. Wondering who this shell of a man was whom Tanis struggled to remember. Like the corpse Tanis viewed in the morgue the day before, at best all her father's caregivers could do was speculate of his identity. Of course, they knew the person in the bed was her biological father, but the soul of that person she once knew and loved remained a mystery to all, especially his daughter.

Tanis called Sandy at home but he was at church with the kids. She spoke briefly with Allison on the phone, remembering their private conversation at a party once when Allison explained why she stopped attending church. She told Tanis that she was no longer able to connect with some aspect of her faith that remained real and accessible. Both women shared a quiet understanding of what it meant to lose that connection, struggling to believe in something bigger than family or work when even those relationships disappointed. Now as Tanis' father lay dying, any meaningful connection with that part of her life seemed so far away.

Allison promised to have Sandy page her back when he got home, but she didn't offer to pray for her and her dad as one might expect. Tanis was grateful that Allison didn't say anything she did not genuinely mean. Allison's unconditional acceptance of Tanis was received as a prayer itself.

★ ★ ★

Sandy stopped at the park on the way home from church to burn off a bit of the children's sugar high from the mini donuts he bought them after Mass. As usual, the kids headed directly for the play structure, getting their dad to follow them up the maze of ladders and ropes too small for Sandy to easily maneuver. His pager went off, but he ignored it. These were the moments he felt most alive, believing in and celebrating the goodness of life even when words failed him. Like his clumsy efforts on the play structure, he equally felt inadequate to express the importance of his family without becoming vulnerable. These were his moments that kept him connected; the very moments Tanis longed to feel again for her own dad, which Sandy instinctively knew must be savoured. They were the enduring moments that would keep family connected to each other no matter what fate awaited them. He saw the grittiness of life everyday but could not allow that world to penetrate what was sacred and real, robbing his children of the gift of a father's presence. He was a good cop and knew how to protect people, insulating the innocent from having to see the darker side. More than his children, however, it was his own childlike wonder that he had to keep intact and alive.

Allison envied this about her husband. Just knowing what he did for a living without hearing all the details was enough to taint her. It was hard for her to always believe in God when so much abuse and suffering existed in the world, especially when she felt some so-called people of God turned a blind eye to it, or even perpetuated the suffering. But for Sandy, it was precisely because of his faith that allowed him to deal with the seediness of life without losing focus on his children. His wife sometimes, yes he'd admit, but never his children.

The pager went off again but Sandy stubbornly refused to let the shadow of work overpower the light set brightly upon his children as they played this morning. They giggled in delight at their dad's hopeless efforts to crawl through the netting and tunnels even smaller than the other obstacles on the play structure. He was stuck in a comical way, but also felt wonderfully free.

CHAPTER 22

Luc drove to St. Benedict's parish to collect. He heard from his sources earlier in the day about Mai Ly's altercation with the priest on the street last night. She did not return and he could care less if he ever saw her bloody face again. But he did care about his interests. It didn't take much to threaten the women who feared him to gather information on this priest; where he came from, and how long he was hanging around his stretch of Hastings or Gore and spending time with Mai Ly. He pulled into the church parking lot that was full of cars belonging to those attending the noon Mass. It had been a while since he stepped in a church back in Montréal, long before his mother was killed, he guessed. He didn't go to her funeral at the church, either. He stood at the back entranceway, not sure when it was going to be over. He studied the priest and watched him going through the liturgy, imagining him in his world far from this pretty little church. He scoffed at those around him in the back pews, looking so pious and hanging on every word their priest said, whereas he knew what the priest did in his off hours.

He pretended to look at the posted bulletins while the parishioners made their way out after Mass was finally over. He kept his head down while paying attention to where Fr. Bao went. He followed him into the sacristy room when he thought the last person left. Another woman remained behind, talking with Fr. Bao when he approached in the door way.

Sensing he was out of place, Mrs. Morrisey asked, "Can I help you?"

"Yeah, I like to talk with the priest."

She looked at Fr. Bao as if to ask, "Are you okay having his conversation with him now?"

He nodded, saying to the visitor, "Sure, can you give me a minute please? I can meet you in the church."

"I'll wait," Luc answered, without moving.

Mrs. Morrisey looked nervously again at Fr. Bao, and he motioned for her to leave; that it was okay. Luc leered at her body as she walked by him, leaving the two of them alone. Luc noticed the red bite mark on Fr. Bao's hand.

"I heard you got that last night from my girl, Mai Ly."

Fr. Bao immediately blushed, looking out through the sacristy door to the main church.

"I heard you got yourself a little present the other night too. Any chance that bitch Magda also left you a bite mark, or was it just your illegitimate baby?" he asked, mocking him.

"What is it that you want?"

"If you've been fucking her you owe me some money, pal. I thought you priests didn't fool around, or was it just altar boys? The girls tell me you've been around the street, buying Mai things, maybe getting stuff for Magda."

"I'm sorry, and who are you?"

"I'm a business associate of those women you were banging. And I'm here to get my cut."

"What are you talking about?"

"I'm talking about you fucking my girls, and now I'm here to collect the money you owe me. I'm sure people would want to know about you hanging out in the Eastside having sex with whores. Although I understand perfectly well. Even priests have got desires, right?"

"You bastard."

164

"Isn't that what Magda left you? A little bastard? Or was it a bitch? Doesn't matter to me. What does matter is you owe me money."

"You think you can extort money from me?"

"I can do whatever I like, and right now you're going to give me my cut for banging my girls."

"Get the hell out of here."

"Hey, I thought everyone was welcome in God's house," Luc taunted.

"Not your kind. You are scum and all you do is make slaves of women."

"That hurts, Father." Luc put his hand to his chest, jeering at him. But then as quickly his smile turned menacing.

"But this doesn't have to get personal. It's business. You use my goods for your little fantasies and then you pay, and obviously your credit is long overdue given how many months that bitch Magda was hiding being knocked up by you."

"She is not a commodity. She's a human being, for God's sake!"

"Aren't I a human being also, Father? You're taking this way too personal. Now, give me my money or I will get personal with you."

"You don't scare me. Get out of my church. Now!" Fr. Bao stared him in the face, unflinchingly.

The colour in Luc's face flushed bright red. Fr. Bao did not notice the telltale signs that the women quickly recognized as time to back down. The priest opened the exterior door of the sacristy to the rectory parking lot, a different door than the way Luc came in.

"Get back to the hell hole where you belong," Fr. Bao commanded defiantly to the man who was not accustomed to taking orders. It was a calculated error.

Luc grabbed the heavy monstrance on the sacristy counter next to him that was used on First Fridays of the month to reverently display the Blessed Sacrament. The radiating metal rays around the altar centre piece in which the consecrated host was inserted were intended to depict the radiating Presence of God. But in Luc's anger, it was a convenient weapon to teach Fr. Bao a lesson, just like he felt he had to teach the women who stole from him. It was business, and from Luc's perspective, he had to make sure both his business associates and his clients understood the terms. If you steal, either by skimming money or a john not paying, Luc exacted payment. In this case, a decision around which form of payment was made.

The monstrance rained down on Fr. Bao, the first blow across his chest, with the metal rays of light cutting deep within. As Fr. Bao's hands went up instinctively to protect him from even deeper cuts, more were delivered to his arms and head. But it was when Luc turned the monstrance in his hand, exposing the heavy metal base and bringing the full weight of it repeatedly down on Fr. Bao's skull and face that resulted in the fatal blows. Luc threw the monstrance down besides his victim's pummeled face and walked out the door, past Fr. Andrew in his car, who had just pulled into the rectory parking stall, seeing a glimpse of the hulking man hurrying past.

Startled and confused, Fr. Andrew went over to the church side door to the sacristy that was left open, seeing the body of his brother priest lying beside the bloodied vessel. The sacred vessel that was used to ceremonially display Christ's glory now bore witness instead to His passion and death.

★ ★ ★

The young boy clutched the scarf his sister gave him after he dropped his sandals during the boat crossing. He had cried as his prized possessions sunk under the waves, oblivious to what everybody else had lost in leaving their country. The entire boat mourned with him, sharing in the tears that glistened down his raw, sun burnt face. The sister's gift to her distraught little brother was a gift to the community, offering hope that despite everything they lost they still had each other.

Now the white silk scarf was filled like a sail as it caught the sea breeze, leading them to shore. The little boy hung tightly to his silk sail as he peered over the gunwale, riding up high in front of the boat as it slammed into the beach. Only then did he let go.

A'nh waved as she emerged from the jungle and strolled down the beach towards him. She was radiant and beautiful, calling out to her brother to join her.

CHAPTER 23

A chorus of pagers and calls all over the city rang out as reports of the incident at St. Benedict's came through. Sandy took his call from home as he strolled in with the kids, having shut off his pager earlier at the park. Tanis answered her first page from the care centre, and then again shortly after Sandy called. Her dad was now cheyne stoking, with further mottling of his arms and legs. The staff told Tanis her dad likely only had hours left.

She still could not find her dad in all this but at the same time could not leave him, either. Ironically, she thought, how absence of any emotion, her vigil was an act of faith. To be a faithful daughter. Mostly she was aware of her mom's presence, smiling occasionally to herself as echoes of her mom's consoling words and touch came to mind. The nursing staff brought Tanis tea and a blanket, turning her dad regularly and providing the appropriate pain medication to ensure he was comfortable. She was well cared for, as was her dad, and now that her mom's spirit surrounded Tanis, she felt a sense of family again that she had not experienced for years. Her dad was dying and would soon join her mother, but she no longer felt she was being orphaned.

Nor did she feel she was abandoning her partner. Sandy repeatedly reassured her to stay with her dad and not worry about the investigation. He just asked that she let him know when her dad passed away, as well if she needed anything. She smiled at that offer, trusting that he was a man of his word. Hot headed at times, yes, but incredibly loyal. It was the other thing Tanis shared with Allison in having one person in her life who stood by you no matter what, even as her dad prepared to take leave of this world.

Tanis inquired a bit about the investigation, reassuring Sandy that some knowledge of the case would help her put her at ease, freed from the distraction of imagining various scenarios of what could be happening, which in her mind was far worse. She always wanted to know exactly what was going on and what to expect, whether about a case, or now, as her father's death neared. She knew Sandy chose his words carefully, insulating her from too much detail as he would protect his own family. All she managed to glean from her partner was that they found Mai Ly. Before passing out, Mai Ly gave a description of the man who beat her, who was now the principal suspect in Fr. Bao's murder based on her statements. This was corroborated by the descriptions both Fr. Andrew and Mrs. Morrisey gave of the man they saw at the parish, including the case for motive that was slowly emerging.

The police were following up on some leads and were confident he would be arrested soon, despite the reluctance of people to come forward to talk. There was a certain code to life on the street. The Downtown Eastside was more a community than people realized. Despite the ravages associated with the Eastside, it was hard for people to leave and upset the delicate order that held people together in tragic co-dependency. It was not so much the availability of drugs that kept people bound to the Eastside as it was the need to ease the collective pain they all shared, which substances and other self-destructive behaviours attempted to numb.

People like Luc also fled a life of their own pain. Without Mai Ly or Magda to channel his anger, or even the Fr. Bao's of the world he felt acted as the arbiter of society's judgment of his sins, he was a nobody. It would take prison to replace any sense of community he risked losing.

But Luc faced a far worse fate than prison, or even death. Sandy paged back later that evening to ask how Tanis was doing. She said her dad was strong, and as the vigil continued, she was surprised how Sandy's question made her realize that something did change as she watched his laboured breathing for the past few hours. She was beginning to feel her dad's resilient spirit again. He displayed a remarkable dignity that held her spellbound, watching each breath he took, punctuated by longer and longer seconds of apnea when he stopped breathing. When the evening shift came on the staff provided more comfort measures to both father and daughter. Whereas previously a page or phone call was a welcome relief from the loneliness of the room, now she was anxious to return to his bedside, becoming more attuned to her father's increasingly shallow and intermittent breath.

Out of respect, Sandy only added that they caught up with Luc. He was hiding in one of his prostitutes' apartments until she managed to flee him when he became drunk. She ran to Stewart's to call police, and the old man let her use the phone only when she frantically threw money at him. Luc pursued her to the store in a drunken rage, falling down in the aisles of cheap clothing racks that she attempted to hide behind. She ran out onto the street with Luc following, trying to grab at her, failing to see the car heading west on Hastings that struck him, hurtling him in the air to the hard concrete sidewalk where he had profited off the avails of prostitution. Sandy said the last they heard he was in St. Paul's in an induced coma to lessen the swelling from his severe head injury. If he survived at all, he may be left with permanent deficits.

"Sounds like his pimping days are over," Tanis added, without wanting to pursue the conversation further.

"Yeah, but he's not the first of his kind who's brain damaged. A lot of them are pretty messed up in the head," Sandy said in an offhand way, also signaling it was time to end the conversation.

"Hey, before you go…"Tanis said.

"Yeah?"

"Sandy, I want you to know how much you mean to me, and how much support I feel from you and Allison. Thank you for that."

Sandy was taken aback, but gracefully acknowledged her words with a simple, "You're welcome." He added lamely, "we've got each other's back."

"Yes, we do."

Tanis hung up the phone at the nursing station and went back to her father's room to spend the last two hours of his life in tender embrace.

CHAPTER 24

Ryan was devastated to learn his friend Fr. Bao was killed. He was in utter disbelief that someone could do such a thing to a man he considered a person of integrity; a holy man. It was in moments like this when he was so demoralized that he counted on Fr. Bao to strengthen his faith, to find meaning amidst senseless tragedy. Now when he needed him most, he was gone. Just like that.

Ryan was not prepared for the ensuing media calls that he characteristically handled with confidence and poise. He stammered when the reporter asked for comment. There were long pauses before he managed to say something intelligible. The Archbishop did not fare much better. It was obvious that the violent death of Fr. Bao had shaken the entire city. Representatives from the various faith communities sent immediate condolences in a clear message of solidarity. The parish of St. Benedict's was in shock and mourned his passing. Flowers and notes started piling up outside the entrance of the church and along the sidewalk by the clothing hamper.

At first, the media were respectful and sensitive, capturing this outpouring of spontaneous grief. But when reporters began probing a link between the two deaths, and allegations of Fr. Bao's association with the downtown Eastside scene, including innuendo of sexual impropriety and even fathering Baby Jane Doe, Ryan fought back.

Some talk radio programs shows started calling the child Baby Jane Bao. Other people came forward saying they often saw him on Hastings or on Gore, buying women things, circling the neighbourhood in his car. His parish community kitchen and outreach ministry proposal was painted by some disgruntled parishioners as a cover for his late night visits to the Eastside, which the assistant pastor inadvertently played into by acknowledging his brother priest's frequent outings. The comment from Mrs. Morrisey, who overheard Luc in the sacristy demanding money from Fr. Bao for using his prostitutes, was particularly damning, raising further questions of embezzled parish funds to support his addiction.

Ryan's defense of his friend in the media and in private conversation increasingly became shrouded in speculation and doubt. The story of a love triangle gone tragically wrong was soon cemented in public consciousness and it made difficult any efforts to dispel the rumours as anything more than an elaborate church cover-up. There was no good response that Ryan could give. Even trying to provide some family history of his immigration to Canada and hardships encountered in the boat crossing and internment camps only served to raise attention to the gangs and corruption among some members in the Vietnamese community. No one seemed interested in exploring his adoption and being raised by loving parents in Manitoba, or what prompted his call to the priesthood. That was obviously not sensational enough. Instead, Fr. Bao became demonized as a symbol of clerical secrecy. Magda was judged a *persona non grata* who brought down both saints and sinners alike in scandal. Ryan lamented how even in death we could abandon people.

Such whispers were not far from the lips of those attending the traditional prayer service the night before the funeral a few days later. Ryan was there, as was Stephen and Marie and others from the parish social justice committee.

"I will miss him."

Marie was surprised at her husband's hushed confession. They had just sat down in the pew, waiting for prayers to begin. The church was already filling up quickly. Stephen glanced at his wife, then nodded to other parishioners in the pew beside them.

"Miss him? I thought you couldn't wait to see him transferred to another parish."

"Shush. Keep your voice down," Stephen said under his breath.

Marie paused, deciding whether to discuss this in hushed voices now, or wait until later.

She simply added, "I am going to miss him as well. He made me think."

Fr. Andrew led prayers for the packed congregation. It took nearly two hours, and Fr. Andrew expected it to be even longer tomorrow afternoon with the Archbishop and all the media present. Hundreds of people from the community were expected to attend. The elderly parishioners paid their respects tonight knowing they would not be able to tolerate the long service and interment at the cemetery tomorrow. The parish volunteers were prepared for this, serving light refreshments downstairs in the parish hall after prayers. It was well after nine at night and still a surprising number of people gathered. It would have been too sad to simply drive home afterwards without some fellowship.

Ryan was there, seeking out mutual friends he shared with Fr. Bao.

"Good to see you, Tom." They shook hands formally.

"Hey, Ryan. Have you met my wife, Wendy?"

"Hi, I'm Ryan Scott. Fr. Bao, Tom and I have spent a few nights out on the town," he said warmly. "I'm the guy who always wanted to go out for a beer after the hockey game."

"Oh, so you're the one responsible for Tom being so grouchy the day after games. He just told me it was because the Canucks lost," Wendy retorted with a smile.

Ryan quipped back, "Oh no, Tom doesn't need me. He's grouchy all on his own. He would be even a lot worse if it wasn't for Bao and me."

"Especially if the Canucks lose," Tom added, smiling.

The warm conversation in the parish hall spread out like a consoling blanket, insulating parishioners from the cold emptiness that lingered on after the service. Other good natured laughter filled the hall, masking the shock and bewilderment many felt. Tomorrow's funeral was expected to reopen their wounds, but tonight they were spared much but the gentle dipping of their toes in the collective pool of grief.

Stephen approached the three and said hello. Marie was already engaged in animated conversation with another woman behind them.

"Hi, Stephen," greeted Tom.

"Hi, Tom. Wendy, Ryan," he said, acknowledging each in turn as he entered their circle.

"How are you, Stephen? I haven't seen you for a while," asked Wendy.

"Oh, you know me, I always have work somewhere."

"No surprise. I think Stephen is on every board and committee known to man," said Tom. "You still on the social justice committee?"

"Yup. That, and Children's Ed."

Ryan added jokingly, "Yeah, we needed a lawyer on our Archdiocesan strategic planning task force but he shot us down."

"You've got to have boundaries," defended Stephen warmly.

Wendy looked right at her husband, "See Tom, how come lawyers spend their nights at home with their family but docs can't?"

Ryan added, "Yeah, and don't say it's because you were doing a delivery."

"It's all a part of an obstetrician's life."

Marie came forward and joined the conversation, her timing perfect to quip, "Oh, don't believe everything Stephen says. Lawyers have strange hours too."

"And priests." Stephen's observation changed the tone immediately.

"How do you mean?" Ryan questioned, with an edge to his voice.

Tom intervened, wanting to avoid conflict, "Well, look at Fr. Andrew... prayers tonight, funeral tomorrow."

"Which is going to be crazy," added Wendy, with the same unspoken need to avoid a confrontation. "I couldn't believe how long the prayers were even tonight."

Ryan didn't let it go. "That's part of the job. But I sensed you meant something else, Stephen. What are you getting at?"

The tension continued to escalate. The laughter in the parish hall seemed to disappear.

Stephen cleared his throat. "Well, there are lots of parish needs right here in our community that could keep any of our priests plenty busy besides work elsewhere."

"Like the Eastside?" Ryan felt his anger racing through his blood. His nostrils flared and he fixed his gaze on Stephen. Besides the amiable chatter in the parish hall that disappeared, now it was as if no one else were in the hall besides them.

"Is that what you mean?" Ryan repeated. He continued, "What Fr. Bao did downtown was as much a part of his ministry as his work here."

"You think so? All I know is he took on so-called projects while other basic parish programs were ignored."

"And you know this, because...?"

"Everyone knew it. If you weren't hiding in your Archdiocesan office you would know it too."

"Stephen," Marie said firmly.

Tom and Wendy saw the gloves coming off and didn't dare say a word. Tom especially knew the third-man-in rule in hockey. Stephen raised the tension ten-fold with this personal shot at Ryan, but he was equally unafraid or prepared to back down.

"It's alright, Marie. Ryan asked a simple question and it's good we set the record straight. All we're going to hear tomorrow is how wonderful he was."

"Stephen!"

"I said its okay, Marie. The truth is, he wasn't around and there are lots of questions about what he was up too."

"At least he was prepared to get his hands dirty and see the reality of life, not just going to tea and crumpet meetings," Ryan shot back.

"Get dirty is right. I'm sure there are a few dirty little secrets in his closet. I think one was left behind on Friday night."

"You asshole!" hissed Marie, with rage in her voice.

"Okay, okay, let's take it easy everybody," Tom interjected. "I think we're all a little emotional tonight."

"Emotion is good," answered his friend Ryan matter-of-factly, while looking steely eyed at Stephen. "Do you want to know what pisses me off?" he continued. "It's when people become narrowly focused on the small stuff and can't see the big issues. Like the social justice needs of the downtown. At least Bao was prepared to address the messy issues; costing him his life."

"Oh, I see the big picture all right. What I see is a priest who preaches justice on one hand while contributing to their harm on the other."

"What makes you say that?" asked Ryan.

"If people have problems with addiction or prostitution, then fine. But don't think you can help them by condoning their behaviour, even encouraging it."

This caught the interest of the physician among them. "How do you mean?" asked Tom.

"From what I heard, he bought prostitutes condoms and coats to keep them warm on the street so they could keep working longer into the night. If he really cared, he would have focused his efforts on getting them off the street altogether."

Ryan was quicker to respond than Tom, but echoed his thoughts.

"Oh, for Pete's sake. You're saying he supported their lifestyle, their habit, just because he wanted to keep them warm, or help prevent the spread of HIV? That's like saying wearing a seat belt perpetuates car accidents, like you're bringing it on."

"You're talking harm reduction," observed Tom.

"Right. Bao was a big believer," confirmed Ryan.

"On that I can agree. He was even talking about having a safe needle exchange programs in our parish down the road," added Tom.

Stephen sighed heavily. "So, let me get this straight. We start with a proposal to open a community kitchen. Fine. But then we're offering public health services, counseling everyone who drops in as a pretext to do what he was really after: encouraging addicts with clean needles."

Marie looked sick. She thought instantly of their own son, guilty for what they did. "You're the one to talk, Stephen. You're unbelievable. You know that? I can't believe what you're saying." She turned and left the group.

Wendy reached to touch her, her hand sliding off her arm. She thought she should catch up to Marie and take her aside, but decided against it.

The laughter and faces in the room came back into focus. Ryan turned to Tom and Wendy and said goodnight, without acknowledging Stephen. He walked over to the coat rack to get his jacket. Mercifully, another couple came up to say hello to Wendy, also pulling Tom into the conversation. For an awkward moment Stephen was alone, both his wife and estranged son a life apart, and his daughter only tolerating her visits home. He looked over at the table where coffee was being served, grateful to spot a friend he knew who could rescue him from the present emptiness, allowing him to contribute again to the uneasy levity in the hall with his own masked laughter.

★ ★ ★

Marie climbed the stairs, avoiding eye contact as others came and went from the parish hall following prayers. She intended to wait for Stephen in the car. "I should just leave him behind," she thought angrily.

The scent of candles hung lazily in the church. A few parishioners were scattered about in small groups, engaged in quiet conversation. Others sat alone in prayer. One woman had obviously been crying and was being consoled by another with soothing words of reassurance. Marie recognized them as friends of Fr. Bao. The meditative stillness in the church contrasted with the din emanating from the hall below. With each step further from the stairwell, Marie felt the calm reaching out to her, softening her anger and exposing the pain she carried. Tears welled in her eyes as she walked along up one side of the pews where it was shrouded in shadow, concealing her vulnerability.

As she came to the statue of the Virgin Mary, she began to sob quietly, holding her forehead in her hand. She lamented all that could have been and the guilt for not trying hard enough, or maybe trying too much to keep her family together. Her son whom she once held in her arms like Michelangelo's *Pieta* was no longer coming back. She was weighed down by her own memories, released with each convulsed sob.

Praying, she whispered through wet salty tears, "Ease his pain, ease his pain," over and over again, like the mantra of a rosary. She reached to touch the statue as though reaching out to her son, Mary's ceramic doe-like eyes interceding in prayer at the woman at her feet. "Be with my son as you are with your own," she pleaded softly.

The heat of flushed cheeks made her tears sting. She reached in her purse for Kleenex, fumbling with her free hand as one hand remained on the statue, in part to remain connected to her son in prayer, as well to steady her frame as weariness of bottled, disenfranchised grief finally found release. The Kleenex slipped from her left hand to the floor below. She stooped to retrieve it, holding on to the statue in which motion automatically swung her body out on an angle, pulling her slightly towards the statue's pedestal base. She grabbed for the Kleenex, turning her head to the side beneath the pedestal where the base met the floor. The long pedestal curved inwards at the middle and then out at the base so that there was a little space at the floor, from which Marie's eyes fell on a small envelope protruding out.

She took the Kleenex, wiping her eyes and blowing her nose, before returning it to her purse and clasping it shut. She let go of the statue and stood back to look for the envelope. Surprisingly, it was not obvious from this stance, imaging for a moment that her tears had impaired her vision. Her curiosity was aroused, helping to calm her. She bent down and this time crouching and leaning her right arm on the wall beneath the statue she saw indeed there was a white envelope nestled in the small crack behind the base along the floor. She reached with her other free hand to retrieve it.

The envelope was heavy but flat, stained by some dark dried blood. It was creased with sweat and immediately Marie understood. It was an alms sacrifice given in prayer. Maybe an atonement. The blood and sweat stains on the envelope were no different from the blood that drained from her own face, and the tears shed for her dear mourned son. She looked up into the ceramic eyes of the statue to see the look of compassion of the Madonna, united in sorrow with Marie and all mothers whose child had been lost.

CHAPTER 25

She stood winching again in pain. Quietly, she opened the door of the confessional and left. One last look back at the bundle on the seat before the door closed for good. Closing a door on a part of herself. She felt warm blood trickling down her leg, and her brow moistened in cold sweat. Magda also knew a door was closing on her life. She reached deep inside for one last, desperate attempt to make right when everything else in her life seemed marked by despair and failure. She steadied herself along the row by holding onto the backs of the pews. Each one offered her strength and support that neither her father nor mother could provide, except Babcia.

She felt each pew with a wet palm, intentionally releasing it as she let go of the memory of every person who abused her, neglected her, and betrayed her. Her father repeatedly molesting her in Poland beginning at age eleven. Her mother, who just stood by doing nothing, even beating her with a wooden spoon when Magda tried to tell her what her dad was doing to her. She learned not to trust, enduring the abuse by making herself small, hiding, not standing out, and meanwhile always looking for ways to escape the pain.

She ran away, thinking it would be over, only to find herself dependent on others when the money she stole ran out. Being dependent and vulnerable, she was at risk of being abused all over again. First relatives, then boyfriends who wanted things, and then the pimps who wanted more. In Poland, and soon after in Canada where she lived illegally the last seven months, it was always the same pattern. Steal from those who hurt you, then flee, leaving behind another part of herself, like she left her baby tonight. Magda protected herself by becoming small like the pregnancy she concealed in blankets and oversized coats. She tried to be invisible, hiding both her baby and the hopes and dreams her unborn child represented.

The pattern meant she would end up in the very place that she tried to escape. Her only family now was Mai Ly and the other women who at least understood her experience. But she couldn't even trust them with her secret. In the end, only Fr. Bao knew.

She let go of the last pew and grabbed onto the statue firmly, taking from her blue coat the envelope stained by blood that seeped through in the confessional. She silently prayed through gasps that her offering may be received. The other hand grasped the statue, as Marie would do less than a week later. Magda held the envelope of money that she stole from Luc to provide for the child. The baby she hid to insulate from the life she knew. To protect her baby from those who would hurt her, more than the wound the child would always carry throughout her life knowing her own mother abandoned her. Would her baby ever realize this? Will she forgive her? Was there redemption for both mother and child?

Magda placed the envelope at Mary's feet where she knew it would be seen once they came for her baby, after she was long gone. But she did not realize the police wouldn't find it. As she turned to leave, wincing in pain, it fell down. It would only be found by a woman who shared her sorrow, who also lived all her life hiding, allowing herself to be made small so as not to push back.

The warm blood persisted, leaving an intermittent trail of blood to the side door where Magda exited the church. Her blood sprinkled the neighbourhood as Magda wandered, crying. Her tears were washed away by the same rain that cleansed the blood on the streets, and what pooled on the

SkyTrain platform upon which she waited later that evening. As Magda pushed open the door to the church, she realized she did not name her baby girl. The silken scarf in her other pocket bore the name of Bao's sister, which was embroidered for all to remember, but she did not even leave behind a scrap of paper with a scribbled note of what to call this baby.

Magda sobbed for what her life could have been and wasn't, for what she dreamed and for the betrayals she endured. She cried alone, as even her own lament was drowned out by the sound of traffic on wet roads. She cried for the years she made herself numb, not allowing life to touch her, until finally, in a side alleyway between Pender and Main, life came forth from her. Life that she had to protect and shield and give away.

The rain fell on Magda, washing away the guilt of her life and for the decisions she made this evening. She opened herself up to the rain to cleanse her and make her whole, walking for hours in the rain until she could stand no more. And still the rain fell like a blessing, bringing peace. Magda accepted that what she did was right, for she saw already the pattern of neglect that she lived under with her family and feared it revisiting the next generation. Now it was time to get as far away from her baby as possible, and at the same time away from those who knew her, who could pull her in again. No, she had to hide, to make herself as small as possible. She boarded the westbound SkyTrain, where within fifteen minutes she would become unconscious, and soon thereafter die from severe preeclampsia and hypovolemic shock, invisible among the evening travelers, destined to circle the route until a throng of drunken hockey fans finally noticed her. Her last consolation was the woman who did not fear her or want something from her. The woman who felt safe next to Magda, weary from a long evening of work. The warmth of her body offered some comfort as Magda's own body grew cold and her life ebbed away.

CHAPTER 26

When the sun shines, Vancouver is one of the most beautiful cities in the world, especially in June. Tourists and locals alike walk or run the Sea Wall encircling Stanley Park and the beaches along English Bay towards Granville Island, a particular favourite attraction, bustling with shops and fresh markets. Real life postcard images of tall ships, glistening glass sky-lines and seaplanes abound. Surrounding coastal mountains with residual snow tops complete the picturesque view. Although a closer look reveals the transient drug user population, homelessness, and haunting emaciated faces associated with the city, when the sun is out, even the seedy face of Vancouver's Downtown Eastside seems less oppressive. It is easy to forget about the violent world of gangs, drugs, and addiction when the sun shines, burning away the mist dampening our human capacity to believe hope is still possible.

On that Saturday afternoon, not many miles from the Eastside and under a bright warm sun, the speeches all conveyed optimism. Even though local neighbourhoods surrounding the park were economically distressed, it was easy to distance oneself from the realities of this part of the city with what went on over *there*. And though Fr. Bao Park, for whom it was being publicly dedicated that day, had recently been cleaned up, the graffiti, used condoms and empty liquor bottles in nearby back alleys were a grim reminder of poverty's extended reach.

When the sun shines down so warmly, we can reassure ourselves that what might happen in this park at night is but an isolated blemish in an otherwise respected working class community. No one need fear that by dedicating the park to Fr. Bao and opening the community soup kitchen at St. Benedict's half a block down the street in honour of the slain priest would begin a downward spiral of decadence. There was no need to fear housing prices would depreciate or businesses close by serving the poor families who evidently lived in the area. The sun and dignitary speeches reassured local residents there was no need to be concerned about what was being acknowledged in their own backyard. Free coffee and donuts and the smell of a freshly cut lawn made more pungent under the warmth of a bright June sky allayed fears that we might be encouraging addiction and homelessness. As long as the Eastside provided a confine for people like Magda to exist far from the tourist sites of Granville Island or Grouse Mountain, there was no need to be concerned that Fr. Bao Park and St Benedict's Community Kitchen Outreach Ministry would threaten local sensibilities. The city needed the Eastside to make us all feel better, to help dispel the gloom.

The Archbishop was invited to speak next.

"I have been asked to bless the park and community soup kitchen," he began, his clear gentle voice undistorted by the microphone. The Archbishop had been well loved and respected over the years for his practical wisdom and lack of pretentiousness. When he spoke, people hung on his words, expecting they would be moved. It was not uncommon for the media to be at loss for their next question when interviewing him, visibly impacted by his reassuring presence that communicated calming hope.

"A blessing... it is indeed a blessing that we have this much needed resource for the community. A blessing to have the legacy of Fr. Bao Luong's work to carry on."

He had no prepared speech, and was in no hurry to end with the perfunctory formal prayer.

"You know, when I first met Fr. Bao, this skinny kid, an adopted immigrant to Canada, I wondered what motivated him to be a priest, what fueled his passion to serve. Who was this man, and what was he all about?"

He paused.

"Oh, I knew he was one of the so-called Boat People. I knew he lost family and went through a lot just to get here, alone and with nothing but the shirt on his back. I suspect not a day went by in his life that he didn't mourn his family. I also suspect that we all want to fill that gap about his life and what he did and what went on inside him. Well, I don't."

He let his words hang. Michelle and André were in the front row. Michelle sobbed quietly into her Kleenex as André pulled her close tenderly with his arm over her shoulder. His cheeks were red but he managed to smile proudly for their son. Fr. Andrew had called his adopted parents to tell them what happened after he found Fr. Bao in the sacristy. He kept them on the phone when ambulance and police arrived so they could be with him before he was pronounced on scene, even though Fr. Andrew knew that his brother priest died while he was anointing him on the bloody floor of the sacristy. The next day, Fr. Andrew drove out to Kelowna to bring them back to Vancouver for the funeral, and a chance to view their adopted son's body. Michelle could not bear to see him so Fr. Andrew stayed with her at the funeral home while André went in the room to view the body. Fr. Andrew stayed close, not only during those tragic first few days, but also during the interval months before the park dedication. He was a tremendous source of support to both of them.

Still, it was obvious to Fr. Andrew how raw Michelle was, having felt she lost her son multiple times in her life; a fate too cruel for any parent to bear. The dedication that served to preserve his memory helped somewhat but Fr. Andrew expected it would be a long bereavement journey for her, even with André at her side.

The Archbishop paused to smile at Michelle and André warmly, conveying in that simple gesture that he would also be there for them, but more importantly, his confidence and that they would endure. André felt Bao was still with them and together, both of them would help Michelle to go on.

"I don't because I look to what he accomplished, the blessing he was to our community and his ministry of service in establishing a parish soup kitchen to meet the needs of others, when in his own life he could have benefitted from an equally compassionate gesture. I stopped wondering about Fr. Bao Luong long ago and instead started believing in him, in his vision, for helping me, his Archbishop, to remember the call of the Gospel to social justice. He is and will always be a blessing in my life."

The message was clear. Anyone who was tempted to perpetuate innuendo further would be measured by what the Archbishop just said. He had a way of laying nonsense to rest. From now on, critics would be asked whether their remarks helped to build the Kingdom of God, or thwart its establishment. The words of prayer that followed were simple and clear, and the ribbon that was cut opening the kitchen and the balloons released in honour of Fr. Bao floating above the park gently punctuated the testimony already given. The sun shone brightly on the balloons as they were carried aloft.

April from the Eastside shelter spoke next, honouring the partnership between her agency and St Benedict's, offering a supportive link to help people who were transitioning from the streets in need of additional community supports in the suburbs and a way forward. Having the community kitchen also helped keep people at risk in the parish neighbourhood from spiraling down a destructive headlong path to the Eastside or elsewhere. She reminded those gathered that the project was never simply about the food or basic intervention services. It was about giving people an experience of hope.

April thanked Fr. Bao for his vision and the anonymous trust money donated shortly after his death that led to an outpouring of other financial support to realize his dream.

Stephen was there, and so was Marie, but they stood apart. Stephen grimaced uncomfortably through a strained smile with the other parish social justice committee members when their photograph was taken. In between pictures and media interviews, other committee members talked excitedly, including Lee, Iain and Peter, and even Linda, who saw possibilities with her business connections in Jamaica to start a similar project in her home country.

Stephen was muted. The Archbishop's blessing had seen to that.

"Good to see you again, Ryan," greeted Peter. "It's been a while."

"A little easier than the funeral, for sure. Bao would be proud."

"Absolutely. I didn't think it would ever happen given the business case but that man had a way of sticking to things. Frustrating guy, to be honest. He wasn't the easiest priest for a Treasurer to work with, you know. Real stubborn," admitted Peter with a smile.

"Don't I know it? Hey, tell me something," Ryan asked.

"What's up?"

"Rumour has it that the seed money for the trust fund was the same money the

guy came looking for when he killed Bao."

"Your point?"

"The point being that some people may have a hard time knowing where that came from. All this good as a result of evil, that sort of thing."

"What do you think of that?" asked Peter.

"I think there is already a lot of good that came from evil. Look at Bao's life. He lost everything, including his life. That's blood money in more ways than one. What about you, being the head of the finance committee? Isn't there some professional obligation to disclose?"

"There might be if I knew about the money. As far as I'm concerned, I don't know about any tainted money. It was an anonymous donation. I don't deal with innuendo or rumour. You heard the Archbishop."

"Right," agreed Ryan.

"Looking forward to your statement to the press, Ryan, should they ask questions."

"We are a church of social justice and 'meeting people where they're at,' that's my media sound bite."

Nicole and Timmy looked up at the balloons as they drifted away. Nicole was upset they didn't get to keep one but Timmy explained that they were sending the balloons to Heaven so the nice priest who went there could have them to play with. Allison and Sandy held hands and smiled as their precocious son tried to comfort his little sister. Since Tanis' father died, Sandy was working a new assignment in the child welfare division that allowed him to spend more regular hours at home, which had made a noticeable improvement in his marriage. Allison saw that Sandy was less irritable and more relaxed and effective in comforting the kids if either were hurt from a minor scrape, getting into a squabble among themselves, or in this case, forfeiting their balloons to Heaven.

Sandy called Tanis after her father died and they went for coffee once, but they both knew that their partnership was over. Tanis said she was not hurrying to return to work, if she did at all; and instead was spending time volunteering at the care centre where her father died. She found it comforting to be there, sensing his presence whenever the sun filtered through the atrium. She read to residents and helped with the twice-a-week family tea. Sandy had made the mistake of questioning Tanis about wasting her time running teas when she could be helping others on the street, but as soon as he said it, he felt ashamed. He knew he was wrong and had no right to say that, which he quickly apologized. Tanis did not react and Sandy never mentioned it again.

They spent a bit more time talking about others at work and how things were going with Tanis in settling her father's estate. In turn, Sandy let her know that the baby girl was being adopted after it was determined no father or next of kin were coming forward. The adopting parents were initiating the process of naturalization, for which Sandy had been required to provide an affidavit. Tanis casually asked about Luc and whether he had progressed since his head injury that delayed police laying formal charges, but she did not ask anything else or show further interest in the case.

When Sandy got up to leave, he gave her a hug, knowing it was goodbye. They had not talked with each other since.

April came up to Sandy and Allison and said hello. Sandy introduced the women to each other and explained how they had met, which Allison took as her cue to step away to let Sandy talk shop. Timmy's patience in mentoring Nicole had run thin anyways, requiring urgent parental intervention once he started teasing his sister.

"I just want to say thanks for all you did for Magda," April offered. "And for organizing her funeral."

"You're welcome, April. I wish we could have done more for her."

"You did. You gave her baby a home, and hope."

"We'll see." Sandy was reminded of some abuse cases involving adoptive parents.

"Are those your kids?"

"Yeah, they're a handful," he acknowledged warmly.

"I can tell! They're nice, and your wife too. You're lucky you have them."

"Thank you. Do you have family?" asked Sandy.

"I do. My girls are my family. We all miss Magda like a sister. We have to look out for each other."

Sandy was surprised at how genuinely April beamed as she said this. Now it was this fiery street worker who gave him hope. Tanis and Sandy had played a part in trying to bring some stability and order in Vancouver's Downtown Eastside but it was people like April who lived among the poor and marginalized and helped forge a sense of community. They were the real heroes, much like Fr. Bao was in his community.

"You should know something," Sandy mentioned. "St. Paul's is thinking about creating a newborn safe haven so babies won't be left in dumpsters or back alleys."

"I heard. And a couple Catholic hospitals in Edmonton are planning to do the same."

"That's good. It provides another option to augment the existing safety net."

"We all need a safety net. I see yours are trying to get your attention."

Allison was keeping the kids from barging in on daddy as he talked work, but was losing the battle.

"Have you been inside to see the community kitchen?" asked Sandy.

"I was there already. They have a lot more food there. Your kids might be interested in what they have to munch on right about now."

"Oh yeah, that's for sure. Thanks, thanks for your assistance."

"Oh, don't be such a cop, Sandy. Go have some fun with those kids. I think he'd want that."

"Fr. Bao? Yes, and Magda."

"Yes, and especially our Magda."

Mai Ly stood off to the side, near the tent canopy that had been set up in the park for the refreshments. She was wearing a summer dress with a small floral pattern. She wore no makeup and her hair was pulled back neatly. There was, however, still some faint bruising where Luc had beaten her. Shortly after Fr. Bao got in his car that night and left the Eastside, Mai Ly overdosed and was treated at St. Paul's but not before managing to tell police of her assailant. After detox, she was discharged and referred for treatment. Once she learned Fr. Bao was murdered and her tormentor was gone, she found within her the strength to start again, despite previous relapses. Since starting her recovery program, she began working part time at the shelter under April's supervision in exchange for her lodging. This was a familiar path that the other part-time staff shared in common, one that April also personally benefitted from, helping to provide a vulnerable person a practical leg up.

She touched the silk scarf she wore around her neck bearing A'nh's initials. After Fr. Bao's death, Sandy had given it to her when he interviewed her in hospital. She wore it proudly. He had returned it to Michelle and André first, but they said he had given it to Mai Ly first, and wanted to honour their son's decision. The Vietnamese embroidery comforted her, connecting her to her own family, which she had begun to reach out to again. As dysfunctional as her story and the many stories of people on the street were, it was funny how she clung to them. Better to come from some family than none at all, she told herself. Still, she felt she knew A'nh through Bao's eyes, who transferred his own feelings of attachment of a mourned sister onto her. While she had walked away from her own family, she had, like Magda's baby, experienced some sense of adoption. A second chance; grateful her parents and sisters never gave up on her, continuing to write and reaching out to her. Her father was saving money to come out to visit her, and maybe even bring her back to Montréal when she was ready. She felt she belonged again. She was more than her English translation of her name. She was Mai Ly.

Marie was there too, also on the fringe of the crowd, looking in. She kept to herself what she had done, not out of spite for Stephen, but for Magda who inspired her to reach out to her own son. The community kitchen was the opportunity to reconnect broken lives and forge a stronger sense of family that she had since with Michael. Stephen did not know, nor did she care. She would no longer live under his shadow.

Marie saw the woman with the silk scarf with her hair pulled back, standing alone like her. She looked beautiful as the sun glistened against her jet black hair. Their eyes met, and they both smiled.

The End

CPSIA information can be obtained at www.ICGtesting.com
Printed in the USA
LVOW08s1332230914

405300LV00002BA/40/P